I0736353

My Lemon Tree
Samantha Barendson

Translated from the French by

Christine H. Chen & M Jaime Zuckerman

SPUYTEN DUYVIL

NEW YORK CITY

© 2017, éditions Jean-Claude Lattès.
Translation © 2023 Christine H. Chen & M Jaime Zuckerman
ISBN 978-1-959556-38-1

Library of Congress Cataloging-in-Publication Data

Names: Barendson, Samantha, 1976- author. | Chen, Christine H., translator.
  | Zuckerman, M Jaime, translator.
Title: My lemon tree / Samantha Barendson ; translated from the French by
  Christine H. Chen & M Jaime Zuckerman.
Other titles: Mon citronnier. English
Description: New York City ; Spuyten Duyvil, [2023]
Identifiers: LCCN 2023012933 | ISBN 9781959556381 (paperback)
Subjects: LCGFT: Narrative poetry. | Novels.
Classification: LCC PQ2702.A744 M6613 2023 | DDC 843/.92--dc23/eng/20230428
LC record available at https://lccn.loc.gov/2023012933

A ceux qui m'accompagnent

To those who walk with me

This is what we share:
An immediate nostalgia for what is past
The melancholic joy of living.
Isabelle Monnin,
Les gens dans l'enveloppe

Apparently, when he died, some parts of my body turned completely pale. Apparently, when he died, I asked my aunt if he was up there sitting on a cloud. Apparently, when he died, everyone cried a lot. Apparently, when he died, a letter was discovered. Apparently, when he died, that letter was thrown away. Apparently, when he died, he'd been sleeping. Apparently, when he died, he'd just returned from Spain and all his trunks were still on a boat. Apparently, when he died, nobody could reclaim his trunks from Buenos Aires. Apparently, when he died, he went to a cemetery, then a garden. Apparently, when he died, he became a lemon tree.

Chapter 1
Forty years, empty spaces

Hace apenas días murió mi padre, hace apenas tanto.
Hugo Mujica,
Y siempre después el viento

My birthday didn't help.

This year I turned forty.

This year my daughter turned fifteen.

My daughter, born at fifty centimeters, three point six kilograms, is now fifteen years old and has a pair of breasts.

This year I still don't have my driver's license, and my daughter will very likely have one before me.

This year I could have died, but all ended well.

This year I gained some weight.

This year it's time to do all the things on the list of things to do before dying.

This year, for the first time, I felt his absence.

I look it up in dictionaries: small, big, classic, literary or encyclopedic. I open them, I check the definition, and I close them again. There's no point, I always find the same explanation. *Father: Man who produced or adopted one or more children.*

The dictionaries speak of creation, of source and origin. They don't say what comes after that. They don't explain what happens when that origin stops.

I did not know my father.

He died in 1978. I was two-years-old. He was barely forty. He died, suffocated in a hotel room in San Carlos de Bariloche, Argentina, at the age when one is still immortal.

I look again in different dictionaries. *Daughter: Person of the female gender considered in relation to her father and/ or her mother.*

Here, again, there's no explanation of what happens if one of the parents vanishes.

My father did not know me.

Yet, the day he died time didn't stop.
He remained my father, I remained his daughter.

A cup of tea got the best of me.

It's a habit I have, seated on the couch at dusk, evening after evening, that triggered it all.

A cup of tea in a life regulated by repetitive actions, the permanence of hot water, seventy degrees, licorice-mint tea bag, white porcelain cup with a poppy, handle turned right and no sugar.

Routine.

A routine in a cup that he'll never know.
And I begin to panic.

I'd like to list everything he didn't know, couldn't know, but all this listing is impossible, and I can only think of examples.

He didn't live through the fall of the Berlin Wall, didn't listen to Madonna sing, the bands Depeche Mode or INXS, didn't read *The Book of Disquiet* by Fernando Pessoa or *Ogres' Delight* by Pennac, didn't watch either *When Harry Met Sally* or *Harry Potter* at the movie theater. He missed the transition into a new century, the death of John Lennon, Michael Jackson, David Bowie. He missed the marriage of Lady Di and the even more decadent wedding of Albert of Monaco. He didn't know the TGV, the Minitel, smart cards and cell phones. He missed all my birthdays.

Apparently, after his death, time and the living have continued moving forward. I, his little two-year-old daughter, became a woman of nearly forty—an age when one's still immortal?

I thought, *what is a habit?*

Movements that renew and return and remake and turn and resemble each other?

A way of stopping time, of letting it slip gently, as if it could be stalled?

The memory of a loved one through domestic gestures?

My tea was none of that. It was nothing more than a need for warmth, a necessity for ordering the day-to-day in iterative moments, a way of avoiding surprises, the promise of traditions, the birth of a long line of hot water drinkers.

And I continue to panic.

Will I spend the rest of my life making tea?

I thought I'd gotten used to his death, that I'd accepted this state of things at an early stage—this situation.

No father, just a mother.

The only daughter of an only mother.

But can one ever truly adjust?

It's likely that my loneliness and his silence were masked by the turmoil and clamor of the other members of the family clan: my grandmother Nonna, my grandfather Nonno, my uncles, my aunts, and my cousins.

Like most Italian families, we heckle at the table, talk emphatically with our hands, sometimes even yell at each other. Nonna always serves the same meal, and we always make the same remarks, the same judgments and the same jokes. Every reunion is like a theater piece that we repeat over and over again. There is tenderness and a lot of love.

I no longer have a father but I have them, my little tribe, my family.

At least, that's what I thought.

Nonno eats breakfast, drinks a glass of red wine, and dies.

Nonna follows him three months later.

Thus, my mother's parents disappear. Vanished. Gone. In a silence that's unlike them.

My penultimate defense against death crumbles quickly, and I become mortal. Didn't see it coming.

My grandfather, Nonno, had admitted he was getting bored. He knew he'd grown old—he was overweight, he could no longer eat the food he enjoyed, especially charcuterie, and had long been forbidden the pleasure of smoking a pipe. His sole entertainment was crossword puzzles and watching television. He said he didn't want to die before his wife so she wouldn't be alone, but he couldn't hold off any longer. He gave in and led the way.

The following months, I went to see Nonna in her retirement home. After Nonno left, she no longer had her entire mind. *Alzheimer's* said the doctor. Sitting on the edge of her bed, I chose a conversation topic that we unfolded over five short minutes, then the timer reset to zero, and we began to retrace the entire identical conversation. Just like in the movie *Groundhog's Day*, I tried to bring subtle changes to my speech, hoping to tilt her back into a dimension where she could talk to me normally and not like the adolescent she'd become who pitied herself because her father wouldn't give her pocket money. The rare times that she returned to reality her widowhood plunged her into terrible sadness. So, I preferred the adolescent Nonna because she was happy in those moments.

My maternal grandparents were both nearly a hundred years old. Their living room wall is evidence of their longevity: a series of family photographs showing up to four generations. Among them a picture featuring Nonna, my mother, me, and my daughter. There, inside a frame, is where I come from in its entirety.

My grandmother brought four children into the world. Three girls and a boy. My mother is the only one who was born in Argentina. The others were born in Italy during the war. She was the baby of the family, who never knew the noise of bombs and the military absence of her father. She didn't sleep in the makeshift bed of a dresser drawer in the cellar. She came after the storm and expectation, on the other side of the hemisphere, in a new land and in a strange language. My aunts and uncle are listed in the Italian family record book. In the Argentinian family record book, only my mother appears. She was always a separate child, loved differently, maybe a little more, maybe in other ways.

And then I was born, product of the baby in the family, child of the youngest, a little fragile thing with big astonished green eyes, granddaughter of Nonna and Nonno.

They were always there. In Spain in 1976, when I came into the world. From 1979 to 1981 in Argentina, when my mother returned to live with them with me in her arms. From 1981 to 1985 in Mexico, when they came to visit in the summer. In the afternoons, Nonna took me aside in the living room and taught me the Italian of our roots while Nonno rested. He always took a nap, even during the war, not a day of his life unfolded without his 120 minutes of rest. Thereafter, his round belly became the preferred spot for the babies he napped with. In 1981, they relocated to Paris, and we followed them a few years later. And when we moved to Lyon in 1987, they didn't hesitate to follow us, very closely, to the other side of the street. They could help with my adolescence and crises with my mother, and welcomed me so often to their guest bedroom, it rapidly became *my* room. They knew me when I was a very little girl, later as a stupid teen, then as a young woman, a young wife, and lastly, a mother. They even watched me get divorced.

Sometimes they annoyed me. Nonna's habit of pouring Orangina over strawberries with sugar. Her way of sighing on the telephone Sunday evenings to make it known she would have liked a little visit over the weekend. *We're old, and nobody comes to see us anymore, it's so sad, this big empty house…[sigh].* Their diverse guilt-tripping techniques, largely inspired by Dan Greenburg's book *How to Become a Jewish Mother in Ten Lessons.* Their insistence on buying me chocolate éclairs, even though I hate them. Their strange way of conversing: I ask Nonno a question and it's Nonna who responds. Their systematic process of replacing names: I'm my mother, my mother is my aunt, my aunt is my cousin, my cousin is my other cousin, who is me. And the corrections in red pen on postcards sent during vacation.

I miss them. I wish they annoyed me again.

They were my family and I asked them nothing.
You always think that you'll have time *later* to ask these questions. It's always too late. Thousands of questions live in us, and we're afraid to be too fragile, emotional, distraught, or troubled by the answers they summon. It should be possible to put their answers in a tin can buried at the back of the garden, to know that these answers exist but can wait for the right time to confront them.

When is the right time?

Certainly not when the whole family is dressed in black in the hideous, apricot colored room at the Guillotière cemetery. Certainly not in the crematorium when the last cells of her brain burn along with her memory partially erased by disease. Certainly not when the pretty red vase was last placed in the columbarium next to a pretty blue vase. Their last love nest.

When is the right time?

My fifteen-year-old daughter tells me, *you're so lucky, you knew both your grandparents.*

I'm so lucky, I knew both my grandparents.

I could have answered, *you're so lucky, you know your father.* But I've learned to stop being sarcastic with children.

My grandparents took with them the answers to the questions I never asked: the names, the places, their memories, and part of my memory. They took away everything except what I believed was the most buried, the history of my father, their almost son-in-law, taken from life too young.

The house now deserted, I enter the attic and realize it had been waiting, mourning. An old grief pervades. Their absence awakens a pain I believed was dormant.

Until then, I believed in fate. My father is dead, it's sad but it has always been that way. The child that I was would have liked to have a father, the adolescent then learned to live without, and the adult put him voluntarily in a drawer of memories as if forgotten. What else can I do? Crying hasn't made him come back, being sad doesn't make sense if I want to move on.

And then I bury my grandparents, and his death suddenly resurfaces and comes tearing up my life, ripping my roots and leaving me with hearsay, empty spaces surrounded by words, silence with noise inside, absences, cravings, deprivations.

It began with a tingle, a minute hollow in the belly, like when I'm hungry. The tingle became a swarming, an itch, an irritation. The little hollow became a trough, a pit. I wanted to glance over the precipice, but I found the terrain steep and the bottom too dark.

I turned around and went to heat up some water for tea.

It's time to ask the living.

Chapter 2
A Tree

Writing can do nothing.
At most it allows you to ask questions.
Delphine de Vigan,
Rien ne s'oppose à la nuit

When he died, my mother came into my room, sat on my bed, and told me the facts as simply as possible. She told me he died in his sleep, that he wouldn't come back, that it was sad and unfair, that I had the right to cry, and she held me tightly in her arms. I have no memory of this conversation, nor of my heartache. From that moment onward, I began to wet the bed.

And his death continued.

I asked questions, but everyone was still too sad and each responded with silence in their unique way. *I don't know, I don't know anymore, I don't remember, all that is too long ago, it's time to turn the page, I prefer not to talk about it, it's too painful, it was a blur, it's sad but that's how it goes, it'd be better to stay quiet, stop asking questions, I don't know, I don't know anymore…*

One day I was told *he's there, in the garden.*

I've never seen a dead body.

Well OK, I once saw a dead bird that fell from its nest, a dead cat that the butcher's son was examining, a dead frog after a smoking experiment conducted by the children at my school, various dead hedgehogs on the side of the road, some stuffed heads of dead boars and dead deer hanging on the walls of mountain village restaurants, dead roasted chickens and dead beef patties, but I've never seen a dead human being.

I didn't want to see Nonno and Nonna. At each of their funerals, I managed to keep busy away from the room where their cold bodies rested. I arrived at the last minute when the ceremony was just about to begin and viewing time had passed.

I'm afraid of dead bodies. I'm afraid of myself, of my incomprehension in the face of a person who resembles in every detail the person it was a few hours earlier. I'm afraid I'd start to shake the body to wake it up, of not understanding this eternal sleep. I'm afraid of not believing in death.

I prefer dissolution.

Evaporation.

The wind.

All those people seated in a circle around the box. They stare at it, all holding their breath, forgetting to breathe for the ascension.

My father sparked.

One day I was told, *he's there, in the garden.*

I looked at the garden of green, where ivy covers three stone walls, the lawn's always well-trimmed, flowerbeds line two sides, a tree I don't know the name of and a lemon tree grow.

I looked at this garden where I imagined drinking tea on the little terrace, this garden designed to be refreshing in summer's heat, this garden welcoming conversation between little old ladies, this improbable garden in the urban heart of Buenos Aires.

I look at the garden, and I remember my father.

Apparently, it can all go into a vase. They call it an urn, but I prefer to say vase—it's more floral. It seems ridiculous to find yourself with this grey ash between your fingers, holding the entire man without understanding how you got there and not knowing what to do. It seems strange to imagine an entire body, the body of a man, his head, his torso, his arms, his legs and all his life, all the skeleton and its flesh, all of his being, suddenly dust. He's placed in the garden's soil, and you say it's like fertilizer and with a little luck he'll become a flower, an herb, or maybe, a tree. You start to water it, which is better than crying, and every day you think of it, you give him a little water. You talk to him in your head or sometimes in a soft voice. It becomes a ritual and a little less sad than going to the cemetery to talk with the stones.

CHAPTER 3
THREE LETTERS, GRINDING TEETH,
AN INTELLIGENT DOG

There is always a little girl
who tries to survive in her own words.
Jean-Marc Flahaut,
Introduction to *La Patagonie* by Perrine le Querrec

I don't remember anything.
Nothing.

There is a before, a black void, emptiness, silence.

Then, there is my aunt who gives me some baby food in a tablespoon, imitating an airplane.

From the airplane, from the baby food onward, everything is clear. Every memory is there, unclouded and pure. The scents from cupboards, people, food. The sounds, songs, lullabies, voices, laughter—everything is there. The colors, the prints, the flowers, the rooms of the house, the toys, the kindergarten, everything.

But before that, nothing.

Complete blackness.

Desaparecido.

For a long time, I thought that he was *desaparecido.*

"Disappeared." For the French, that word evokes nothing particular, a man goes to buy cigarettes, never returns. Whereas *desaparecido* for the Argentinian, the Uruguayan, the Chilean, that means confined, locked up, tortured, assassinated, totally erased. As if he had never existed.

For a long time, I thought that he was *desaparecido.*
But apparently, he died in his sleep.

I begin an enormous job. An investigation. I will search for my father, reconstruct the puzzle of his life, compile an inventory of who he was.

I sit at my desk, a walnut desk I inherited from Nonno. I screwed a wooden doorstop on each foot to elevate it—I don't understand how my corpulent grandfather managed to write his business mail or work on his accounting for hours at this low desk without knocking his knees. I often work at this table where the surface is ruined in places—notches where he got annoyed with the stapler, grooves where he dug with the cap of a pen while reflecting on something else, wood worn where he placed his forearms, ink stains. I want to work this way, in his thumbprint, in the little menial traces of his past existence. Is this all there is that the dead leave the living? Ink stains?

I sit and ask myself *What do I have? Memories? Things? Some hearsay? Real accounts or family mythology?*

Not one memory of him. He could have been a casual lover in my mother's life—it wouldn't have changed anything for me. Apparently, we lived together for two years. I have some proof: some letters, photos that keep the memory alive. You look at a photo, you think you can remember, you forget, you look again, so on and so forth. I don't have a single memory of him and the photos keep quiet, staring at me in silence, showing an image of a miniature me in the arms of a handsome young man I know nothing about. Where did our existence in these first months go? Where did our childhood go? Can you talk about life without memories?

I can't find a single word, a single smile, a single image in the well of my brain.

He must have spoken to me.

He must have sung something to me, a lullaby, a silly song, hummed a tune.

He must have given me something to eat.

Tickled my belly.

Caressed my head.

Held me in his arms.

I don't find the slightest crumb of memory in my head filled with details, telephone numbers, passwords, lists of things to do, names of unimportant people, bureaucratic protocols, but not even the tiniest spark of a past together. Two years of life together, twenty-four months disappeared. Into nothingness, oblivion, and the wind.

If something exists, you can find it on the internet. If someone is important, they have a site or a blog on the web. If a book is published, its review is online. I do my shopping without leaving the house, and things just get delivered to me. I don't have to do anything, no carrying, just click and its mine. I'm part of this connected generation. I'm part of the information era. My father: no. In his time, the internet didn't exist. So, if I type his name in the navigator, nothing comes up. I appear in his place—my page, my blog, me. I exist, and he does not. According to the internet, nobody comes before me. I come from nowhere. I belong to a generation of orphaned internet users. I keep searching online and end up finding other family members: a few lines in the official Mendoza newsletter about a company founded by my paternal grandfather and his wife; Nonna's identity card number, who, according to the Argentinian site, is still alive and seems to exercise her right to vote; a book titled *Las Cosas* written by my uncle Alessandro, available at a Dutch bookseller; another book titled *Perfide Annate* by my great uncle and available on eBay; a few footprints on the white web of the internet.

Search hard enough, everyone exists, the dead as well as the living.

Everyone, except my father.

Apparently, my parents left Argentina for Spain on a boat in 1975, a few weeks before my birth. Wedged at the bottom of my mother's belly, I knew nothing of this exiled crossing, not the name of the boat, not how long it took, not the weather. Argentinian Maritime Lines closed its doors and sold its last six ships in 1997. I only know that one of the ships, the *Río Tunuyán*, took sixteen days to complete the crossing. It left the port of Buenos Aires, had a layover in Santos, Brazil three days later, arrived in Rio de Janeiro two days after that, took another eight days to cross the Atlantic to stop at Las Palmas de Gran Canaria, and finally, after three more days, reach Vigo, in Galicia. The ship then went on to Le Havre, Hamburg, or London and returned to Buenos Aires. Were they fleeing the political regime, or did they only want to change their life? Did they travel on the *Río Tunuyán* or on *Cristoforo Colombo*? Did they experience big swells, storms, gales or a smooth ride on a tranquil ocean under a baking sun? How many others left with them on the same boat? How many took to the sea so as not to die at the hands of the military? Did they share a little of their history in those sixteen days?

I would like to know the name of the boat. That would be a beginning—my beginning.

I found three letters typed on airmail stationary. They came from Spain. I didn't actually find them. They have always been there in a plastic sleeve where I keep documents having to do with my father. My aunt Claudia gave them to me a long time ago, but I'd never had the courage or desire to read them. They aren't originals, just photocopies my aunt made. She's the archivist of the family—she doesn't keep everything, but she at least has enough memory to answer questions when you ask. In these letters, my father addresses his sister, Beatrice. They're letters from the front. He doesn't dare return home. As he writes on the typewriter, he feels a hollow in his stomach. Argentina is under dictatorship.

In the first letter, he initially says that everything is going well. Then the tone changes and everything is going badly. He talks about the bar that he and my mother kept in Sitges, near Barcelona, of their bankruptcy, of the savings that are no longer enough to pay the rent, of the things they had to sell to buy some milk, of work he hopes to find, of hope that doesn't feed them. Hunger is there and lingers in his words. He asks if she'll send him some provisions, some clothes, a bit of money.

At the end of 1977, they move to Madrid to find work. They don't have a single penny in their pockets. They sold everything and were always hungry. In the second letter, he says he landed a job at SEAT, the Spanish car manufacturer. He says he was hired as a salesman, that he never sold a single car in his life, but it'll allow him to rent an apartment, eat, and breathe again. I am certain he put on a gray suit, knotted his tie, kissed my mother on the mouth and me on the cheek, and then...how many SEAT 1200 Sports did he sell?

Each piece of information brings up a new question—and another question always follows.

The last letter is dated December, 1977. For the occasion, he drew in marker a fat cat dressed as Father Christmas. The letter says nothing special, but some passages shake me.

My daughter is more beautiful each day…
My daughter is silly. She escapes from her crib, and when I scold her, she bursts into laughter...
My daughter is a love, and she gives me so much joy. We spend a lot of time together. Physically, she looks very much like me, but she has a shitty temper…

I am *his* daughter.

He is *my* father.

It's a good start.

I say *my father.*

Apparently, my father ground his teeth.
I grind my teeth.
My daughter grinds her teeth.

For three generations, our jaws have made unusual grindings, squeaks, and other gnashings that troubled the sleep of our roommates, waking them up with a jolt from dreams filled with insects and sweat. I inherited a masticatory habit, eccentric bruxism, his habit, his sound in the night.

The same eyes, the same smile, the same oval face. The sketch of a movement utterly similar, an expression, a shadow, all that is fleeting, uncertain, impalpable. And yet, when the entire household wakes up, annoyed, feeling the night vibrating, thinking everything is going to collapse, and finally realizing it's nothing but me, who grinds her teeth...there, with the rhythm of a cricket, at two in the morning. There is no doubt, I'm my father's daughter.

At the time, my parents couldn't marry because he was already married and divorce was forbidden in Argentina. He was married to Maria G., an older woman he loved but who didn't want children. He wanted them, lots of them. My brothers and sisters were never born, prematurely aborted, destroyed before they were even imagined. I'm an only child, and I'm illegitimate. If he had lived longer, he would have been able to divorce in 1987, and I could have become a legitimate daughter. The language of the law hurt us sometimes. From being illegitimate, I went to orphaned, and with his death, my brothers and sisters never came to be.

Illegitimate and orphaned, I was registered in nursery school where I learned to write my name and several other words. I never wrote *papa*, I never said *papa*. I want to, but I have nobody to say it to, nobody fitting this lovely word with its twin syllables, two soft, occlusive, bilabial consonants.

\'pa. pa\.

Pa-pa.

Pas de papa.

No papa.

However, when my mother made an alphabet noodle soup, a soup of letters, I wrote this word in my spoon, away from all the other letters, far from any other lexical possibilities. I wrote *papa* in pasta. I watched it floating in my spoon in the midst of grease circles. I watched these four letters turn and put themselves in reverse to form its variations: paap, dada, pada...and when I'd played enough with my tiny papa, I swallowed it.

I go through several pages before writing the word *papa*. I don't often say this word, and I surprise myself to write it here, this simple, yet foreign, word. At most, I write *father* because I've never spoken to him. I talk about him only in narration. I say, *my father was Italian, my father died in 1978 in Argentina, my father met my mother in Buenos Aires, my father worked at a travel agency, my father left to live in Spain with my mother, my father and my mother kept a bar on the beach in Sitges, my father had two brothers and two sisters.* I never say *papa*. *Papa* is childish. *Papa* is for when he's right there in front of you, and you can touch him and tell him *here, look, Papa, I got a 20 out of 20 in Italian. Papa* is to tell him, *I love you, Papa.* To say to him, *you piss me off, Papa.*

I often tell him *you piss me off, Papa.* I say it to him in a low voice, in my head, never aloud. There's no need. If he hears me, he hears what's in my head, even if sometimes I speak to him in French, and he didn't understand French. *You piss me off, Papa. You piss me off for leaving so early, for leaving my mom all alone. You piss me off for never being there when we needed you, of still not being here.* He doesn't even take the trouble to enter my dreams. I'd like to wake one morning after a night dreaming of a conversation with him, a stroll, a shared moment. I tell him *you piss me off, Papa. You could have at least come into my dreams. We could have at least spent some time together, gotten to know each other, and my dreams could mix with reality, and then I'd at least have some memories. But no. You piss me off, Papa. Che stronzo, Papà.*

Then, there was this Big Guy in my mother's life. At the time, it was still too soon when she told me, *it would be nice if you called him Papa.*

I tell him, *you piss me off, Papa. Who is this Big Guy anyway? Why do I have to call him Papa?* I tell him *You're my papa, I only have one Papa, living or dead. I don't understand.*

Big Guy stayed, he didn't leave. He settled into our day-to-day, replaced him or thought that he replaced him. Big Guy called me his daughter, filed documents that gave me the status of "daughter." Big Guy wanted to be my new papa.

And me, I was four-years-old, and I didn't want it.

I played with language to avoid saying the word. I spent my childhood dodging the term. *I will not say "Papa!"*

I ate alphabet soup, I played with words, I obsessed over the phrase.

I also made a very tiny label of "Papa" on a ballpoint pen that he'd owned. The pen was in a case. The pen was his body, the case his grave. I glued on a headstone that said "Papa."

Big Guy noticed the pen, saw the label, laughed, and asked me *Why is my name written on a pen?* I answered, *It's not you.* He tells me, *I don't understand, who is it then?* I sputtered, I tried to make him understand, I told myself that he's an adult, that he must be more perceptive than that. He went on asking, *but if it's not me, then who is it?* I wanted to scream, curse, yell at him. It's crazy to be so big and to understand nothing. I told him it was my other father, the one who's dead...there was silence, discomfort, coldness, and my papa became the other—the roles reversed, the world ends. I didn't want Big Guy to take his place. I wanted only one papa. My papa. *You piss me off, Papa.*

I hid myself. People saw me as playful or mischievous. I disappeared to the back of cupboards, under tables or behind sofas, in dark corners, at the bottom of my bed, in old delivery boxes, under sheets hung as tents or teepees. I grew up in the reassuring shadows of nests I constructed for myself. As if afraid of the dark, I came to know myself in the shelter of these places, far from the adult world that could only be reached by voices and smells of mothballs, tomato soup, soap, fresh mown grass, eucalyptus and tobacco. In my hiding places, I could talk to fairies, to God, to ghosts, to my dog, Lucky, or to my papa.

Lucky is a very intelligent dog. He's lucky to have met my father, to remember him. He could tell me about him. Lucky is a red cocker spaniel with rough fur, except under his ears where I pet to help fall asleep. Lucky doesn't know how to talk, but he understands. We communicate using telepathy. He tells me what he knows. I confided my secrets to him. It wasn't until I was an adult that I consented to *lend* him to my daughter. I assume they converse. I assume that Lucky tells her about me, what I was like when I was little, the stupid things I did—he knows me well. She slept and held him tight, very tightly, and her hand caressing the ears of this old stuffed doggie who guards our family's stories.

I'm afraid of the dark. Hidden deep under the covers of my bed, not a single part of my body pokes out from beneath the sheets except for the tip of my nose and two nostrils to breathe some air. I'm five. I'm convinced that a monster sleeps under my bed, waiting for the perfect moment to eat my toes, my ears, anything that's not covered. I roll myself up in the sheets and breath through a very small hole. Sometimes, I hear noises, some words, footsteps, groaning, crying, laughter, and all these sounds that terrify me—a trickle of cold sweat runs down my spine. My nights are short and restless. I wake up more and more frequently in sheets wet with pee or tears. And this dream returns each night:

I'm at the Lafayette Galleries decorated in red, green, and gold from floor to ceiling. It's Christmas and the Galleries are swarming with happy adults and astonished children. I feel good, someone takes me by the hand. We go towards the elevator to ascend to a higher floor. I'm very proud to push the button. The doors to the elevator open and I go in first when suddenly the doors close and the elevator climbs to another floor. I'm alone in the elevator, I'm very small, I don't know what to do. They abandoned me. I cry. And I wake up in tears.

I believe in the afterlife. The little girl who sat next to me in class told me, *if you're not baptized, you don't have a soul.* I grew up doubting everything, but I believe in the afterlife. I need to know my father is somewhere. He needs a house, a place to sleep, a cloud where you meet the other members of the family, the ones in the black and white photographs, the ones from long ago.

I watch movies where the dead linger on Earth in the midst of the living to complete some unfinished business, take some time to say hi to the people they love, and pass on to the other side after seeing a soothing white light.

I learn later that in real life, the dead die in their sleep and don't even know it—they pass directly to the other side, forgetting to say hi to their loved ones. And we're left here, with our esoteric films and televised series.

Once a year, the school teachers insist on inventing gifts for Father's Day so that their cute students can build, tinker, cut, paint, paste, and then proudly give gifts to their sweet papas when they get out of bed in the morning. Poems by Maurice Carême, camembert boxes painted and glued with elbow pasta, drawings of rainbows, potted plants and other wonders—nothing is too good to celebrate papa. During this time, the fatherless children can go about their own business or participate regardless and offer their gift to another member of the family, an uncle, brother or even their mother.

My mother accepts my presents without saying anything and gives them on my behalf to Big Guy who thanks me. I clam up.

I don't like Father's Day.

CHAPTER 4
EIGHTY-THREE SECONDS

I am afraid of an unknown voice
on the telephone who tells me of a death.
Katherine L. Battaiellie,
J'ai peur

When I was ten years old, the year 2000 was an improbable sci-fi future when you could fly in cars, tele-transport or call someone and see them on a screen.

Now, I call my aunt Claudia via Skype. She lives in Florida, and I cannot help being surprised at seeing her on my screen, talking to me as if we were in the same room. Together we drink *maté*, laugh. I take her through my apartment, show her a newly acquired painting, a new cushion for the couch or the view from my window. I love these moments of intimacy that are no longer impossible because of distance, the bad quality of the landline, or the cost of a long-distance call. In the 1980s, the price of an international phone call was so high that we barely had time to talk, *Good morning Auntie, we are doing well over here, we love you, send me some pictures, talk to you very soon, kisses.*

Of all my aunts, Claudia is one of my favorites. I think it's because she's a little eccentric. For a long time, she was an assistant to her magician husband. As a child, I was fascinated by seeing her cut into three pieces or pierced by swords. She's very religious, but she's lived in a nudist colony for several years. I've never asked her if the parishioners went to church naked. Sometimes, she's sad she never had children, but she takes solace in giving all her effervescent, boundless, and exuberant love to her nephews and nieces.

One evening, we were sitting in our respective kitchens, a drink in our hands. She was talking about her dog, Snoopy, who has been doing much better since he's had surgery, and suddenly, it clicked. I waited for a few seconds, and I asked her innocently, *do you have a recording of my father's voice?*

I imagined two responses. The first one, negative, disappoints but doesn't disrupt the order of things as they are now. The second one, positive, suddenly crushes me: my father's voice, finally addressing me, the child from the past and the adult of the future. *My daughter, if you are listening to this recording, it's because I am dead…*

My aunt says she'll look, she might have *something*.

My aunt records everything. When she bought a portable tape recorder, she started recording it all: people's voices, songs from the radio, her dog's yelping, the audio atmosphere in her neighborhood. Instead of letters, she sent me tapes of her talking about her life and the road trips she went on with her husband in North America. I never failed to recognize the brown envelope in the mailbox that always contained a tape and photos of her in short, sequined miniskirts.

My aunt records everything. When she came to visit, she had me stand in front of the table where she placed the tape recorder and asked me to sing. I sang my mother's lullabies, I sang the nursery rhymes I learned at school or songs by Emilie Jolie, and I then made up radio broadcasts, made-up news and invented weather forecasts—the weather was always beautiful.

I wait. I check my mailbox. I wait for her email messages with mp3 file attachments.

She's going to look. She may have *something*.

I want to hear my father's voice. I don't want to be disappointed if my aunt doesn't find something. I want to know what his voice sounded like. She's not going to find anything, she'll find a box full of tapes, the tapes were water damaged in the basement, there was at least one; her husband recorded some jazz over it, his voice was recorded, his voice wasn't recorded, there's a trace of him alive, there's none. What good does it do, he's dead. I want to hear it, I'll never hear it. If I hear his voice, my memory of him will come back, I'll never know if his voice is hidden somewhere in my memory. I have to hear it, it's too late, I want to hear it, it's always too late. Will she find it? And what if she doesn't find anything?

While I wait, I decide to listen to my tapes again. It takes me a while to find them. Since the arrival of the CD, the tapes have been archived in my mother's basement. I end up recovering an old shoebox behind a pile of boxes, after moving a garden table, a life-size wood cutout of the Tex Avery wolf, a wicker lawn seat, and three chairs. Among the tapes of U2, Depeche Mode, Lloyd Cole and the Commotions, Pink Floyd, The Beatles, Vangelis, Simon and Garfunkel, there are about thirty of my aunt's tapes.

My old cassette player is still in my daughter's bedroom. I sit on the floor, while my charming daughter enjoys making fun of me.

The recordings are a series of questions my aunt asked: *How is my favorite niece doing? Are you working hard in school? Did you make friends in class? Do you like your teacher? What's your favorite food? What's your favorite color? Do you play sports? Which sport? Do you get along with your girlfriends? Do you have a dog? A cat? Do you ride a bike? You wear a bra already? Tell me...*I suppose I answered all these questions in the tapes I sent back. I should have done the opposite, asking lots of questions and waiting for the answers...

I wait.

She's going to look, she might have *something*.

His voice.

His voice finally arrives by mail, copied on a CD, expedited by my very tech-savvy aunt.

The recording only lasts one minute and twenty-three seconds.

I press the play button.

From the speakers, his voice booms out, filling the living room and decades of silence.

His voice.

I hear my father for the first time.

I knew his face, the color of his skin, the spark in his eyes. I knew crumbs of his life, some facts, dates, a few stories, but not his voice, which I hear for the first time, recorded.

In forty years, I've never considered asking, *what was his voice like?*

His voice never had to respond to questions, doubts, or blame. I could have turned to his voice for advice, but always the voice stayed silent. His voice is dead, suspended, offline.

His voice comes out of the stereo, while I slowly slip to the ground and place my ear on the speaker, while my body goes limp, my strength weakens, while I notice tears flow down my cheeks, and I realize that I miss him, that he exists, that he speaks in Italian.

His voice.

I listen to it again, once, twice, three times.
It's a lot, it's not enough.
Now I want images with movement.
A musician friend sent me his last recording, made entirely from clips of Super 8 movies that his father filmed when he was a child.
Why don't I have any film of me when I was a little girl? Why didn't anyone film my father at a wedding, a party, in the garden doing a pirouette?
I ask my aunt in vain.

There are only these eighty-three seconds.

1, 2, 3, 4, 5, 6, 7, 8, 9, 10, 11, 12, 13, 14, 15, 16, 17, 18, 19, 20, 21, 22, 23, 24, 25, 26, 27, 28, 29, 30, 31, 32, 33, 34, 35, 36, 37, 38, 39, 40, 41, 42, 43, 44, 45, 46, 47, 48, 49, 50, 51, 52, 53, 54, 55, 56, 57, 58, 59, 60, 61, 62, 63, 64, 65, 66, 67, 68, 69, 70, 71, 72, 73, 74, 75, 76, 77, 78, 79, 80, 81, 82, 83 seconds of him.

And that's it.

A mundane conversation.

And that's it.

The sound of my father.

And that's it.

It's a conversation between my aunt and my father. They speak Italian. A little girl runs and laughs nearby. My aunt already told me this child isn't me.

At first, I don't really understand what they're talking about. They discuss numbers, payments, loans, calculations. At first, I don't find that interesting.

From listening again and again, it finally clicks in my head. The scene clarifies. The dialog makes sense.

My aunt, who records everything, wants to buy her first tape recorder. She's with some friends who already own one. She's trying it out, testing it before she invests in one for herself. Tape recorders are expensive, she wants to pay in installments, she's calculating how much she can afford each month. She's asking my father for advice, who seems to encourage her to buy one.

This conversation on tape in Italian is the genesis of all the tapes to come. But this tape remains the first and only recording of my father. Of his voice.

Apparently, my parents spoke to each other in Italian.

He must have spoken to me in Italian.

I feel silly when I turn to the clouds or to the lemon tree and speak to him in Spanish.

I try to speak to him in Italian sometimes, but it's less natural. It's the language of my grandmothers, not really mine. It's the language of our cooking, of pasta, pastries, olive oil, onions, flour, the language of black and white photos, old stories, dresses and hats, of the scent of hair gel, powder on the cheeks, the language of memories, of tenderness, of fireplaces. That can't be his language.

Other times, I speak to him in French, and I realize that he never learned French—he's never had reason to, and if he were still here, I wouldn't be speaking French either. We'd be speaking Italian together.

Did he smoke? What kind of cigarettes? American, Italian? Doesn't matter, I don't like cigarette smoke. I'd be annoyed if I were sitting here having a cup of coffee with him and breathing all his smoke. No chance that would happen. I imagine him smelling nice, but he may have smoked like a chimney, a pack a day—maybe he had smoker's breath, yellow teeth, who knows. After all, he was apparently a player—he loved card games, poker, betting. He loved drinking, partying, going out with beautiful women. He loved getting all dressed up and being well-put together, like a dandy. So, for sure he must have smoked—a smoker of long cigarettes or cigarillos. I would have fought with him over his cigarettes. *You piss me off, Papa, with your cigarettes.*

I would like to lay my head on his chest, tell him, *you stink of cigs,* and lay there anyway to find his scent buried under the smoke, the scent of his skin, of his hair. I close my eyes, I'm in his arms, like a little girl in love with her papa.

I know nothing of him, yet it's I who is the blood of his blood, the flesh of his flesh, the child of his sperm, I who is his progeny, I who look so much like him, I who find the shape of his face in myself each morning in the mirror: his eyes, his brows, his nose, his mouth. It is I who carry his name and immortalize him in my poems. It is I who think of him, speak to him, yell at him, and water him. His mother, his sisters, his brothers, his first wife, his friends, my mother, everyone knows more than I do, I who sprang from his source.

I need to question those he spoke to, who heard his voice.

CHAPTER 5
A CAT, TWELVE GLASSES, SIX PHOTOS

I found the pack of cigarettes
my father smoked, and I told myself
that he died between the eighth
and the ninth cigarette.
Fabcaro,
Carnet du Pérou — Sur la route de Cuzco

When he died, our belongings were still on a boat from Spain. After two years in exile, my parents and I, still a baby, returned to Argentina by plane, but the furniture, paintings, dishes, and trunks filled with our clothing, our things or memories, were on a boat that reached the dock a week after his death.

Customs didn't want to hear about it. The trunks were under his name, he died, the trunks stayed with customs.

By the time they plead their case with certification of their passports and request letters, the trunks had disappeared, allegedly seized by customs. Most likely, the contents were plundered by the customs officers, by the dock workers, a shirt taken here, a piece of jewelry there, a toy for someone's child, a painting for a wife, and whatever was not taken was forgotten. Why insist? In totalitarian Argentina, it's difficult to insist with officials.

My aunt Claudia thinks it's divine intervention. God preferred that my mother not keep any material memory. She said this to console me—I should be satisfied with the irreversible choice that God made. Whether by divine intervention or by a customs officer, it's the same: the trunks are gone and with them my father's past, his life, my heritage.

Nonetheless, I inherited a cat.

A Cheshire Cat, like in *Alice in Wonderland*, purple with white spots.

This cat wasn't sequestered by the customs officers—it was in Argentina with some friends who gave it to me years later.

It dates 1968. My father painted it and signed it on the lower right corner. The background is brown, the frame is gold, the cat smiles from ear to ear. The cat is more lilac than purple with white cloud-shaped spots.

I received this cat one Christmas evening. He was all wrapped up. I was told, *Here, open it*, and I cried.

The brown background was hideous, the gold frame too. The purple cat wanted to move out. I painted a background with stripes, pink and cream, and I painted the frame in apple green.

It's a psychedelic painting.

We painted it together, my father and I.

I also inherited twelve glasses.

Colored and cylindrical glasses.

I went to my aunt's friend's place. They gave me a shoe box and told me, *Here, open it*, and I cried.

I drink often from these glasses. I'm afraid to break them because they're all I have left of him, but I want to use them so he becomes a part of my life. When I see a glass of the same style in garage sales, flea markets, or antique shops, I buy it. Each purchase adds to my collection, reminds me of him and diminishes the likelihood of breaking one.

Today, I have fifty-nine glasses.

I also inherited an acrylic turtleneck sweater, blue and worn out. When I was given this sweater in a plastic bag, I was told *Here, open it*, and I didn't cry. I thought it was really cool. I thought this vintage '60's sweater went so well with my new hippie look—it matched my bell-bottoms, my round John Lennon sunglasses, and my long hair. I was sixteen. I thought it was a beautiful thing to wear a sweater that once belonged to my father. I thought of its meaning, of time, of all the things that brought joy and pride wearing this sweater, even so worn out. And I put it in the washing machine.

My father's scent must have been soaked into the sweater, and I didn't think of plunging my nose into the knitting to find the slightest molecules of him that could still remain in its weave. I washed it and his scent, a speck or trace of him was rinsed away with the detergent, displaced by the water down the drain, the pipes, the sewers, the rivers and the sea.

I thought of all this much later, much too late—it's always too late—while I was enjoying a panaché on the balcony of a café overlooking the Old Port of Marseille. Boats swayed gently, fishermen sold fish, tourists walked with their jackets in hand. It was warm for the season— seagulls waited for the fishermen to lower their guard, cyclists rode by, and Our Lady of the Guard kept an eye on the port and the sea, where some nanograms of my father could still float.

I have exactly six photos where we're both together.

In the first photo, in black and white, he's standing next to my uncle Alessandro and my pregnant mother. The photo is slanted, everyone laughs, there's a bicycle behind them. Properly speaking, I'm not in the picture, I'm inside, and they seem happy to know this.

The other pictures are in color. I'm still not in the second picture, but he's wearing a bib and biting a pacifier between his teeth. The photo makes me laugh, even if I find it a little silly.

The third one is badly framed—I see half his face, half of mine, my mother in the foreground, and everyone crowded on the bed in pajamas. It's morning, but who's taking the photo?

The next one is a little blurry, old, and has an orange hue. I'm running naked on the grass, and he's trying to hold me so I won't escape.

In two other photos, I'm in a baby carrier on his back—I smile. I was told I stole everything within reach and hid my bounty at the bottom of the carrier.

Six photos in twenty-four months. And still I don't have the slightest memory of him.

Some answers hide behind their questions.

For my tenth birthday, my mother gave me three albums where she had glued photos of me in chronological order of my birth, my childhood, my school years, and our vacations. In the first album, titled "Spain," the first photo is so small and discolored, I almost missed it. My parents are on the bridge of a boat. She's wearing a turquoise shirt, he a t-shirt with a drawing I can't discern. The image is blurry and enlarging it didn't help. No computer, or scanner, or photo editing applications can process the image to become what it was. Without thinking, I peeled the photo away, flipped it over and read, "Trip to Barcelona aboard the *Eugenio C*—November, 1975."

Apparently, they travelled to Spain by boat. On board the *Eugenio C*. I know the name of a boat, the first notes of my history.

Why am I so moved to know the name of this ship? Is it because naming things makes them more real? Is it because I imagine this vessel that transported 1,636 passengers may have saved 1,636 people from the horror of the dictatorship? Is it the knowledge that I travelled on this boat in my mother's womb? Or simply because I'm proud to know that my parents crossed the Atlantic on the largest ship ever built in Italy at the time? 217.40 meters long, 29.03 meters wide, 14.70 meters high and a speed of 27 knots which is 50 kilometers per hour. Or is it the nostalgia of an era that no longer exists now that we can cross oceans by air on much faster and less comfortable planes? Why am I sad when I read the word "dismantled" in the technical record of the vessel? Why do I have this damn song in my head? *Love, exciting and new, come aboard, we're expecting you…*

I feel the compulsive need to lift the plastic film from every page of the album, peel each photo off the page to find other written words, other clues. I don't find much, some dates, some names of places, but not of people, as if my mother thought we would never forget their friends' names, as if friendship never knew forgetting.

When I ask her about the names of the people in the album, she says *I don't know, I don't know anymore, I've forgotten.*

In this same album, a void is invisible to the naked eye. On the first five pages, my father is present. On the sixth, he's no longer there, he's disappeared from our lives, from our photos, and no one thought of leaving a blank page to commemorate his death.

The end of our stay in Spain and the beginning of our lives in Argentina are on the same page. On the left page is Madrid, on the right, Mendoza—no transition whatsoever. On one side, a little two-year-old girl, on the other side, a three-year-old child, both with the same smile and the same joyful expression.

You don't see anything unusual. The pictures don't

mention his death or his funeral, and you barely notice his absence. Nine months and ten days passed between the two periods. Two hundred eighty-three days when neither my mother, my aunt, or my grandmother was capable of taking any photos. My father disappears, and it's as if we cease to exist in the albums, annihilated with everything inside this temporal parenthesis, forever sealed.

Was this parenthesis a mourning? What made my grandmother, then my aunt, and finally my mother takes up the camera again? The first shot of this new period is of me in a striped sweater, sitting on the ground on a street in Mendoza with a bag of chewy fruit candies between my hands, *Sugus*. I laugh, I have candies, there's color and sweetness in my life. Did the laughter of this child inspire them to realize life deserves to be seen and preserved?

Let's summarize. An acrylic turtleneck sweater, blue and worn out. A sleeveless checkered sweater, blue, red and cream. A silver bracelet made from a broken watch on his wrist in one of the six photos. A wallet with an ID and a business card. A dozen drinking glasses. A purple and white Cheshire Cat and another smaller one that appeared a few years later. A few letters. A silver ballpoint pen but with no refills. A CD with an mp3 recording of his voice speaking for barely more than a minute. A photo album titled "Spain." Six photos of my father and me. And that's it. Not even enough to fill a suitcase, barely enough to fill a page…

I feel the need to fill the emptiness with collections. When I was ten, I collected bottles of Chianti, the ones with a fat round base wrapped in a wicker basket. My mother demanded I stop this absurd hobby after three bottles. When I was twelve, I began a collection of cows that lasted six years. It started with a blue bedspread printed with Sandra Boynton's cows. The bedspread gave me the idea of a birthday gift to a classmate, who, in turn, gave me a mug, after the mug, another mug, then a stuffed cow, some postcards, plates, two t-shirts and so on. When I was eighteen, my dorm room seemed like it was spotted with black blotches on a white background. I finally gave it up because this collection wasn't really me. When I was twenty-five, I began a collection of sand. Whenever I went to a beach or the desert on vacation, I saved a sample of sand in a vial—black sand, white sand, gray or tan sand— but the vials just collected dust. For some brief periods and at different times of my life, I've collected pins, stamps, perfume samples, advertising postcards, stickers, books by Anaïs Nin, and hippos from Kinder surprise eggs.

Nowadays, I collect shopping lists that I find on the street or at the bottom of the carts in supermarkets. A shopping list is like a short poem—it contains the essential of what must be said, a brevity tending towards perfection, the universal. Behind the list of ingredients, there's Nana's recipe, a love of cooking, a pressing hunger, or a TV dinner. There's the empty refrigerator and cupboards to fill, chores to do, things to finish, there are houses, apartments or studios. There are various writings on these wrinkled bits of paper, in ballpoint pens or pencils, careful or shaky handwriting: an identity, a family.

Chapter 6
An earthquake, a fox fur coat

She doesn't even know what she's
looking for in all these things.
Annie Ernaux,
Les années

And then I'm left with all the times he wasn't there. Not there when I lost my first tooth, not there on my first day of school, not there when I banged my head on a swing, not there when I wet the bed, not there when I drew a little man with ten fingers on each hand, not there when I rode a bike without training wheels, not there when I had to wear braces, not there when I kissed a boy for the first time, not there when I had a fever, not there when I got a bad grade in math, a twenty out of twenty in Italian, an hour of detention, not there when I snuck out of the house at night, not there when I went to a nightclub, not there when I came home too late, not there when I had an abortion, not there when everything returned to normal, not there when my daughter was born, not there when I met my husband, not there.

Did he like to cook? Did he know how to dance? Did he sing in the shower? Did his feet stink? Did he like to swim in the ocean? Was he left-handed? Did he wear reading glasses? Did he read? Did he make paintings other than Cheshire Cats? Did he smoke pot? Did he play the guitar? Did he wear bell bottoms? Did he look young for his age? Did he drive a car? Did he love Buenos Aires? Was he funny? Was he strict? Would he have let me go out? Would he have been protective of me around men? Would he have scared away my boyfriends? Would he have liked my boyfriends? Would he have loved me?

I ask my family questions, but they don't answer me. I ask again, they smile at me, they tell me I'm vivacious, curious, playful. They try to turn my attention to other things, other questions, painting or photography lessons, horse-riding or taekwondo or volleyball sessions. They want to keep me occupied, they want to channel this curiosity into something practical.

They divert my attention until the day when the Big Guy brings home a television. I'm six years-old, maybe seven. I turn it on and immediately the screen captivates my attention. It talks to me like a normal person, tells me things, tells me about life, sad or happy, tells me of thunder and storms, doesn't lie, tells me of death. Television becomes an addiction, a drug I take before school, after school when the adults eat out, when they're not taking care of me. I get drunk on images. I want truths.

It was only much later, with my nose stuffed with snot and my eyes red and swollen from crying over the end of my first love, with Lucky in my arms, that I realized TV can also lie.

I spent the summer when I was nine in Paris at my grandparents' home. August was hot, and they took long naps in the afternoon while I watched the TV show *Croque-Vacances*. The two rabbits, Isidore and Clementine, became my friends, I fell madly in love with Captain Future, and I dreamt of being adopted by a millionaire like Arnold and Willy.

The rest of the time, mostly Nonna kept me busy. Mornings, she liked to take me to the museums—I dragged my feet, but I had no choice. Evenings after dinner she insisted on giving me Italian lessons. At the living room table, she corrected the homework she'd assigned the day before and dictated a passage from a book which I had to write flawlessly.

The summer passed smoothly. I escaped, sometimes to the closet that smelled of mothballs, or behind the bed where I kept my dolls. I didn't often hang out with other children, except Francois, the neighbor's son, who was two years younger and wanted to play doctor.

One evening, the doorbell rang. My grandmother asked me to go open the door. I saw my mother on the landing. It had been nearly a month of living with my grandparents, and I didn't think I'd see her before my return to Mexico where we'd lived for the last five years. I was happy about this surprise, this unexpected moment, and I wanted to give her a hug. And while my arms stretched out to squeeze her tightly, I noticed the pallor on her face and the firmness of her lips that told me she was exhausted and needed to rest. She came into the apartment, followed by Big Guy, and they had only two trunks.

They left suddenly, just like that, on the first plane. It wasn't until much later that I found out this escape involved a debt for a large sum of money and a man named Shlomo. The next day she told me, *we're going to live here, in France.*

September 19, 1985, we're still living with my grandparents and on TV, millions of miles away, I watch an earthquake in Mexico completely destroy everything.

They left everything on the spot, books on the shelves, food in the fridge, dirty clothes in the laundry basket, plants in their pots, Q-tips in the bathroom trash. They only brought a few possessions, some photos, their toothbrushes, and they got on the plane.

Then the earthquake in Mexico finished the job of destroying everything. The apartment shook, vases fell, rolled, and broke on the floor. Flowers wilted onto the floorboards. Books also fell, undulating dominos of paper, upsetting the alphabetical order. The plates played a last high note before becoming dust. Ironed piles of clothes became soft mountains. Toys rolled. Furniture rearranged itself. Paintings scraped semi-circles into the plaster. Walls cracked. The TV exploded. Records slipped out of their sleeves and splayed on the floor. Windows shattered, glass covering the ground.

The earthquake destroyed everything—I know, I saw it on television.

My life is made of lost things. From exiles and relocations from countries and continents, my family tree weaves and unweaves according to the dead and the living. Our trunks empty and fill with things that get lost, misplaced, destroyed, or replaced with other things symbolizing the moments we want to hold onto. How many things did we lose with each move? What was in the trunks that customs confiscated? What was lost between Buenos Aires and Sitges, between Madrid and Bariloche, between Mendoza and Mexico, between the earthquake and Paris, between Paris and Lyon? What things survived travel, time, and circumstance? Which things did we purposely lose to forget? Did these things hold our memories?

What's the truth? What's a memory?

My mother never remembers—for a long time now she's shut the door to memory. She sobbed, cried, spent sleepless nights disbelieving. She finally slept, only to wake up to the feeling of his presence and realize his absence all over again. She cried, more weakly, more sorrowfully, she felt broken. She wanted to believe it was a terrible nightmare. She wanted to cling to a single hope, something magical or mystical, and when it didn't happen, she cried and took this old sweater, which she held and buried her nose into it and found his scent in the weave, cried more than ever. She found innocuous traces of him: a grocery list, an old movie ticket, a toothbrush. She felt this heavy sorrow at the bottom of her stomach, this inescapable sorrow, indescribable, this emptiness, this loneliness. Did she learn how to forget so she could continue to live?

Sometimes I think my mother's memory is like a collage. Randomly cut fragments of memories rearranged to produce new ones. Pieces from others' memories come to join these new memories.

I question my mother, then my aunt, then my grandmother. I'll then have three very different versions of the same story, and yet, I know that each one of them is true. I ask about everything, knowing the answers will be partially tarnished by subjectivity. In my mother's case, that happens through her forgetting or ellipses.

We each battle grief as best we can.

The questions without answers from my childhood surge up again in adulthood. I try to balance their weight as they rush at me. I don't have a plan or a structure, nor do I know what I'm looking for. Was he tall? Was he short? Did he like animals? Did he go to museums? Question marks punctuate all my sentences, and my family is forced to answer them, first with tenderness, then irritation. I carry myself like a five-year-old kid who strings together a series of *why's*, who tugs a sleeve to get noticed and demands attention to ask questions again and again. The adults get tired—they want to resume their lives in the present, quit being interrogated, quit having to travel back in time, quit digging the dry earth of the past. I insist, but they end up sitting at the edge of the ditch and leaving me to dig by myself. I find nothing but ashes.

When I ask questions—*Who was he? What was he like?* —they adjectivize. They tell me *funny, kind, caring*. They tell me *Italian, sexy, brown hair*. They tell me *charming, confident, willful* or *stubborn*. They don't tell me anything in actuality. They never talk to me about his skin, his guts, his odor. They never tell me his flesh or his blood. They describe the human, never the animal. They forget his body—his body becomes ashes, leaving nothing but the shell, the appearance, the memory of his smile and his beautiful clothes.

He liked clothes, and he paid close attention to his look. Those who were lucky enough to know him recount that he was obsessive, that his closets were filled with clothes carefully ironed, arranged, and organized by categories. He spent a good portion of his money on his wardrobe, and he was often broke. He didn't feel good unless he knew he was well-dressed, impeccable. He liked to go out evenings to chic places, to cafés on the big boulevards of Buenos Aires, to the casino. Like his father, he liked to play, gamble and, like his father, he didn't know how to stop. He must have had dreams filling his head, dreams of who he could have been if he had money, dreams of luxury, dreams of tailored suits, of convertible cars, of fur coats, of jewelry. To be so close to a dream and unable to achieve it. Another bet, the last one, luck will finally turn. But no, luck never turned, and the part of his salary that wasn't invested in clothes ended up at the casino bar and on the green felt. He must have won a few times because he ended up buying a fox fur coat.

In 1960, Luchino Visconti shot *Rocco and His Brothers* with Annie Girardot. In 1963, *The Leopard* with Claudia Cardinale. In 1970, Franco Prosperi filmed the opulent Anita Ekberg in *Il debito coniugale*.

I learned from my grandmother Liana that Massimo Franciosa, her brother, worked in the screen adaptation of all three of these films. My father was fourteen, seventeen, and twenty-four, but that didn't trigger any desire to be artistic. He didn't decide to get into film, nor did he decide to become a writer, and nothing indicated any relationship between his love of beautiful women and the shooting of these films.

She also told me that he didn't like to read. Nobody could remember seeing him with a book in his hands. It makes me a bit sad to discover this divide between my father and me. *You piss me off, Papa.*

Chapter 7
An airplane

Not always, but sometimes,
I remember that.
Melchior Liboà,
L'amour est blessé par les mots
des chansons qui portent la folie

My partner worries seeing me constantly checking my computer, returning to it compulsively as if a rubber band pulls me back. He calls me Paddle Ball. He says it with tenderness and humor, but I'm annoyed. I know he's right—it doesn't matter whether I receive a new photo or an answer to one of my many questions from my aunt now, or in an hour, or even tomorrow. However, the pull is stronger than I can handle. I check my email on my phone in restrooms—I check again, discreetly, when I get a glass of water. I get up a little earlier in the morning. I need to be glued to my device, something will come up...but what?

Something came up.

The *something* is a new photo from my aunt, a photo I've never seen before. The photo is a little damaged by the sun, the thin film on top of the picture bubbles and cracks in places. My father sits sideways on a leather chair in the foreground, his hand on a steering wheel. Behind him, the window of the cabin shows an air field where I can see a small plane and a palm tree. My father wears a plaid shirt like a Canadian lumberjack, but he's much thinner. At first, I thought he was sitting in a car. I don't know anything about mechanics or cars from the 70's, and nothing resembles a car more than an airplane without wings. But looking closer, the car looked strange—the steering wheel was more like a handle, there were four dial screens, not two, and most importantly, the car was on a tarmac.

My father was a pilot!

My father was a pilot…

I imagine myself at a cocktail party, an evening book launch for a talented writer, a dinner between friends, and suddenly the question, *what did your father do?...My father? He was a pilot…*

Silence.

Respect.

...but he's dead.

Silence. The image of a handsome man in an impeccable uniform in an immaculate airplane that flies the azure Argentinian sky, but then, suddenly, he decides to cross the Andes, and that's when the unexpected and irreversible happens. The crash. Death. The hero.

Respect.

My aunt Claudia tells me he got a pilot license at the National Institute of Civil Aviation at the airport in Morón, Buenos Aires.

Enlarging the photo, I can see the inscription N9509A on the airplane in the background. I learn from my friend, the aviation enthusiast we call the Captain and his collection of airplane catalogs that it's a Cessna 170A, a tourist aircraft with four seats and a single motor built by Cessna from 1948 to 1956. I immediately search images of dashboards from this model, but no, it's not the airplane my father sat in.

I then remember another photo that I hadn't initially paid much attention to. I go through the album, dig up another box where I'd thrown other pictures and then I find it. He's there in the photo, young and smiling, with the same plaid shirt, standing in front of a palm tree, a lawn, and five aircrafts.

On one of them, I can read N3015P. The Captain tells me it's a Piper PA-23 Aztec, one of the first tourist airplanes with two motors, built by the American Piper Aircraft company from 1959 to 1982. I upload images of the dashboard on my screen. There's no doubt, my father piloted a Piper PA-23 Aztec.

I now know that my father can fly a plane at 340 km/h, climb up to 6100 m altitude, and carry aboard up to five people.

He could have taken me all the way up there, and I would have been afraid and would have fastened my safety belt tightly and made a silly laugh. We would've flown together above the Pampa where the grazing cows become minuscule brown dots—we would've followed the curb of the Tigre River and glimpsed the wealthy mansions, we would've spent this time suspended together, far from everyone else, just him and me and the sky.

He was handsome, very handsome. In the photos, he emanates something sensual and elegant. His green eyes are streaked with gold, his chestnut brown hair curls around his oval face, slightly angled by his jaw. Sometimes, he wears a moustache like in the 1900's, sometimes clean-shaven, but always smiling, charming, irresistible. I realized only recently that he was very seductive, the type of man I'd have been attracted to. But now he's younger than I am. And he's my father. And he's dead.

I've never slept with older men. So, I won't feel like I have the Oedipal complex. So, I won't get lectured about how I'm searching for my father, filling the void of his absence. I carefully ignore the older men and go out with boys my own age. They are often too young, their maturity lags behind mine, and I find myself with frail, hairless bodies with barely any muscles, round and smooth jaws, small dicks. Meanwhile, my chest and hips show the shape of the woman that I already am, and my suitors, my lovers, look more like little brothers to me than boyfriends. And I am bored. But I have to resist and refuse to let myself fall into psychoanalysis, giving fuel to morbid gossip—I will not sleep with a man who could be my father.

A few days short of turning eighteen I found out I was pregnant. After those few days, the legal grace period ended—it would be too late and I'd have to keep the burgeoning baby. A few days short of turning eighteen, this little thing in my belly is nothing, a little spermatozoid mixed with an egg, a viscous, lifeless thing, a nothing. A few days later, it would become a fetus, a baby, a human being. A few days short of turning eighteen, I decided to get an abortion. To get an abortion a few days short of turning eighteen means I have to go to a Family Planning Center, be ashamed, have to explain, find excuses, listen to the unjudgmental lady and feel there's a solution, have less shame, listen to the lady suggest I forge a letter of parental consent, listen to the lady suggest stealing a parent's ID paper with the signature, make an ultrasound appointment, listen to the doctor say that the viscous thing is alive and that we can hear the heart, ignore his words, tell myself that this man is an asshole, make an appointment at the hospital, write a fake letter from my parents, forge the signature, steal a passport, go to the appointment, have a stomach ache, wait in the waiting room with ladies over forty, go into the room, forget the procedure and conversation, fall asleep, wake up, go back home, hope that one day it will be the right time, but not now, not a few days short of turning eighteen.

I ended my pregnancy on my own terms. I ended my boyfriend's paternity without his choice. I feel guilty, yet it has nothing to do with him. What does it mean to be a parent? What does it mean to be a child? How do you return the order of things? Later, my daughter will be born, she will have two parents who will get divorced but who are alive. Later, she will have questions about the invisible grandfather, and I can only give her my uncertainties and my love.

At eighteen my father ended his studies and went to work for the airline Braniff in Peru. He stole a vase in a restaurant that he gave to his sister. That's all we know of his time in Peru.

Before he met my mother, he married María G.

There are nine María G's in the white pages, fifteen on social media, and who knows how many more living in anonymity.

I don't dare call them—I contact only those found on the web.

I look at their photos and eliminate teenagers, the ones who are too young, and the ugly ones. My father loved beautiful women, very beautiful women.

Out of the fifteen women, two remain, and one likes flying.

I send an email message, a bottle into the sea, and I wait.

No response.

Nothing.

Now, I have two questions:
Who was my father?
Who was María G.?

No wedding picture. No trace of this first marriage. No wedding dress, no church or ceremony. My aunt who attended the wedding tells me, *her family is weird*, followed by a silence that says a lot without saying anything. No one knows anything, or they don't want to say anything. I am at an impasse, a mystery, a fog that wraps around María G. Is she still alive? Is she dead? Did she just exist in name only? Nothing can prove her existence and, even less, her marriage with my father whose life becomes more and more of a legend. The facts fade the more I dig and whatever answers I get lead to more questions.

Who was María G.?

Does she even know he passed away? Did my message stir any memories from over thirty years ago? Does hate or resentment last through the passage of time? What was her wedding dress like?

CHAPTER 8
A BED, A HOTEL

People who look for their father will always be
the most miserable and often victims.
Eliette Abécassis,
Mon père

One day, he returned to his country which was controlled by the military. He could have fallen into the jaws of the wolf—he might have died a victim, a hero, a martyr. The military might have tracked him, followed him, caught him. He might have been persecuted, tortured and electrocuted. He might have become a *desaparecido*. But apparently, he died in his sleep, far from violence, in the comfort of the Hotel San Carlos de Bariloche, the "Swiss Argentine," in a silent fog of nocturnal monoxide gas.

At 1 p.m., seeing that the two men hadn't settled their bill and checked out on time, the chambermaid entered to ask why. After knocking on the door three times without response, she inserted the key into the lock, a little nervous about dealing with people who skipped out on the bill. Expecting to find a bedroom empty of men, bags, and shampoo samples, she turned on the light and found two sleeping bodies. Two dead bodies when she noticed the strange odor. She got out of there, unsteady with shock in the midst of the stench.

It doesn't make sense.

Just after returning from Spain, he found work in San Carlos de Bariloche, 1,650 kilometers from Buenos Aires. With a partner, he was going to manage a tourist resort that was then under construction along Lake Nahuel Huapi. It was a golden opportunity for these two young fathers. The building site was ongoing, and the bright future of his dreams was of real estate and mass tourism.

And they died.

I found two photos of the building site that my father took. You can see some vacation condos, all identical, between groupings of firs. On the ground, still rocky and dusty, a parking lot takes shape. Scaffolding, a cement mixer and cinder blocks complete the scene. They were supposed to manage the construction, get ready for the next season. They knew it'd be a lot of work, that it wouldn't be easy, that they must be invested in it. They didn't regret their effort and, that evening, they returned to sleep in the hotel.

And they died.

I don't know if the tourist resort still exists. I don't know if the hotel where they slept still exists. At present, there are 125 resorts in Bariloche, and just as many possible crime scenes.

At 1 p.m. a strange odor coming from the neighboring room prompted a woman to call reception and report it. The manager got up and, after knocking on the door three times without answer, inserted the key into the lock, a little nervous about finding addicts. Expecting to find two groggy men, he turned on the light and discovered two sleeping bodies. Two dead bodies after he finally noticed the foul odor. He got out of there, unsteady with shock in the midst of the stench.

It must have happened like that.

There was no investigation. Just an article.

In a country where the military drugged young people and threw them alive from airplanes and helicopters into the river or the ocean, in a country where more than thirty thousand people disappeared, in a country that locked up pregnant women and left them to give birth with hands and feet shackled, in a country that murdered women, men, journalists, nuns, painters, students, workers, writers and poets, in such a country, why would it matter if a tourist resort contractor died in his sleep without justice?

Someone cut out, saved, and photocopied the newspaper article. Who did this? I don't know. It's not very long—in a few lines it summarizes the life of a travel agent. It lays out some facts, saying that he died in his sleep, in a hotel, as result of a radiator gas leak. The article says, *On July 30th, he returned to Argentina to manage a new hotel in Bariloche. A few days later, he met with an unfortunate end.*

Lamentable end, the original article in Spanish says, but I reject the literal translation. His death couldn't be lamentable. It calls for pity, but it doesn't deserve the contempt or disgust implied by recent usage of this empathetic adjective which has become pejorative. It's an *unfortunate* death—every word has importance.

The article doesn't say that there were two in the same room, two colleagues traveling for business. In the photo accompanying the article, only he is there—his colleague is not. His colleague's daughter will not have an article cut out, saved, and photocopied to keep her company and give her answers.

I often ask myself who was this other daughter who lost her papa the same day as me. This other child who lost her father on Tuesday, August 14, 1978, this other child who was partially orphaned, like me. I've often wanted to meet her, find the name of the person who shared the same hotel room and death. Find his daughter, to talk to her, to tell her what? It's stupid to imagine the same causes could have the same effects on different people. I always imagined her as a reflection of me, like a sister, like she could give me all the answers. In my head, I've imagined the meeting and the conversation between these two little girls with a shared destiny. Does she also sometimes think of me? Is she also dying to go to Bariloche to scream at the top of her lungs and spit all her hatred towards the irresponsible and criminal owner of the hotel? Is she also sad when night falls?

Her father was named Carlos F. Ortiz Bilbao.

This name eventually appeared on the screen in a short article that my aunt sent.

It's an insert appearing in the local paper. *TIG (Tourist Investment Group) regrets the loss of two friends, two excellent professionals: Carlos F. Ortiz Bilbao and Franco Barendson.*

The other little girl is named *something* Ortiz Bilbao. Two names as common in Argentina as Martin and Gauthier in France. I continue to lose her trail.

Franco Barendson. I realize this is the first time I've written his name. My father, my papa, my paternal figure, my biological parent, my old man, also had a first name.

In Italy, he was born Francesco, in Argentina he became Francisco and very quickly Franco. When I was little, I really loved his first name and all its variations. For a long time, I thought the general Francisco Franco was a nice man because he had two of my father's names.

Since I began searching and finding the trail of his past, this name has taken up space in my life. I feel less and less like an orphan and more and more like *Franco's daughter.*

Chapter 9
A Document

My father, it's me in death.
Tania de Montaigne,
Toutes les familles ont un secret

I plan to ask his mother, my grandmother Liana.
I bought an airplane ticket to cross the pond, *el charco* as they say over there.

Before this trip, I never gave her warning. I took the flight, touched down, showered, bought a bouquet of flowers in one of the many kiosks along the street, and I rang the bell. "Good morning, a package from Europe," I'd say via the intercom and the maid would come open the door and almost faint when she realized that I'm there without any advance notice. She'd make me go on tiptoe and announce a "big surprise" to my half-blind grandmother who eventually recognized my voice. A smile.

And then someone told me surprising a ninety-five-year-old lady like that is a bit risky.

So, this year, I gave advance notice.

For a long time, she didn't want to talk about him—she was too sad.

And then one day, she agreed to take out the photo albums.

I've always known her as old, but I've always only known him as being thirty-two.

In the black-and-white pictures, she's the one who's thirty-two and he's just a child.
I've looked at all these albums, she's described everything, told me of the past, of her life before, of all his firsts, of the vacations, the affairs, the loves, the heartbreaks.
I thought I'd remember everything, that I only needed to listen and her stories would be mine. But I forgot them.

I forgot everything Liana told me on my trip last year.
I should have written it all down while she talked about her childhood, her youth, her marriage, the birth of her children in Rome, of crossing from Genoa to Buenos Aires on a boat in 1947, of her new life in this far away and foreign country.

I keep going back to the image of my father on the beach. In the minuscule black-and-white photo, she gave me, I see him sitting on the sand, facing the sea—he wears knit swim briefs. He's blond, his hair curly, and he can't be more than three years old.

That's all there is.

I've forgotten all the rest.

I planned to ask her again, to take notes this time.
And this morning, I received an email message.
In English.

I read on my screen that there may be now an unrecoverable silence. Three phrases in English, harsh, and throaty.
She can't speak, can't walk, and cannot recognize people.

Three short phrases in this cold language so that all the family members scattered to four corners of the world can understand: Buenos Aires, Rome, Lyon, Amsterdam, Asunción, Miami or Paris.
She can't speak, can't walk, and cannot recognize.
She cannot speak or walk. And she doesn't recognize anyone anymore.

For now, words are silenced—memory is closed.
I can't ask her anymore.
My library is slowly burning, and I haven't finished reading the books.

Soon I may have another vase filled with ash that I pour between my hands to the earth and hope will grow another tree.

It's always too late, I should have thought of it sooner, when there was still time—time was there and life was ahead of us, but so were procrastination and excuses. I don't have time, there's so much to do, work, commute, my girl and her homework, house chores, grocery shopping and exhaustion, and let's do this tomorrow, let's have a cup of coffee first, we'll wait until the weekend, wait for the beautiful days, wait to be in shape, wait to have the courage, wait for the moment, the right moment, the suitable moment that doesn't come, that never comes, and it's too late, it's always too late.

I know it though.

I know I delayed my reply to my uncle Alessandro's letter. And my uncle died.

I know I delayed my call to my literature professor. And my professor died.

I know I should have asked my grandmother. And my grandmother is about to die.

Why do we wait? Why is it always too late?

A friend tells me he wants to record his mother. She just moved into a nursing home. He would like to interview her about the past, the family, and force her to talk. He's hesitant. I go with him to play the role of journalist, like someone who doesn't know anything and asks questions. My friend records everything. It's not always too late.

I saw a French movie. At the end of the movie, the husband dies of cancer. A week earlier he inflated a balloon. His widow finds the balloon, deflates it slowly and breathes her dead husband's air, his departed breath, his last breath of life. I cried my heart out. Just like every time I think of the dead, of the shapes their elbows leave in their sweaters, of their cups of coffee abandoned on the kitchen table in the early morning before they left, of the hollow on the mattress, of messages left on answering machines, of their scent on nightshirts shoved under the pillow, of their toothbrushes, of all these signs of life that remain long after.

In a letter my aunt Claudia sent me when I first started this investigation, *when we saw your father for the last time, he said to me, "who knows when we'll see each other again!" After he left, I burst out in tears, and I wrote a note: "Is it possible that he was telling me he was going to die?"*

My aunt is a very spiritual person who sees signs and meanings around her. While her mother, Liana, can't talk or walk or recognize anyone, my aunt worries about where my grandmother's soul has gone off while her body is here but empty.

I suppose that my father wanted to say simply that they will not see each other anytime soon because he was going to live in Bariloche. I also believe my aunt cried because she was moved to see her brother leaving for the opposite corner of the country. Imagination and grief did the rest.

What's the point of continuing this investigation? It's too late. Too late to ask the right questions, too late to meet the right people. I'm circling around and around. Time is doing its job of eroding, the footprints of the family memory washed away by waves and wind. I suppose this means the journey reaches its end. Apparently, when we die, we die. I have searched so long, dug, rummaged, interrogated. I come back to his absence always, to his disappearance.

Though my father has a voice now, a face, a checkered shirt, a pilot's license, and a vase, his life is more like a painting by Braque, a collection of disparate images that try to tell a story. My story, my collage.

Neither one of the María G's has replied.

My grandmother finally found her memory after fifteen days of blackout. She completely recovered her voice. *She can speak.* My aunt believes its divine intervention. The doctor talks about a cerebrovascular accident—the artery unblocked itself, Liana came back to herself without any side effects. But for how much longer?

In two months, I will return to Argentina. Will she wait for me? Am I going to arrive there again with my questions, my doubts, my empty spaces? I don't know.

The photo albums are still at her home, on top of the armoire in the guestroom.

The stolen vase from Peru sits on a shelf at my aunt's home.

The Cheshire Cat smiles above my bed.

The sweaters don't have any more scent.

A lemon tree grows in Recoleta.

In the end, the only document that conveys an objective perspective of his existence is the death certificate. I got the 1978 original and its French translation in 1981. I've had to present this document several times to the city hall for various administrative procedures that demanded proof of my identity: *I was born in Spain of an Argentinian mother and an Italian father who's passed away. No, I'm not Spanish, I was born Italian, and now I'm also French due to my mother's marriage to the French Big Guy. I grew up in Mexico, but no, I am not Mexican, and no I don't have the same last name as my mother or the Big Guy, my last name is the same as my father, the one who passed away in Argentina. No, he was Italian, yes, I'm French. What do you mean, it's not possible? What do you mean, there's a missing document?*

Excerpted from the death certificate:

According to Article 70 and 80 of the Civil Code: I certify that on page 21 of the registry number 250 of the duplicate copy of the Vital Records book of San Carlos de Bariloche, corresponding to the year 1978, volume II, is found inscripted the death certification of: Francisco Barendson, of Italian nationality, holder of the identity card number 4003560, death occurred on August 15th, 1978, at Bariloche. Son of Antonio Barendson and Liana Franciosa.

Prepared upon request of interested party to present to whom it may concern; I am mailing the present excerpt onto which I am affixing the seal and signing as a public officer of the Vital Records of San Carlos de Bariloche, on stamped paper.

In San Carlos de Bariloche, the thirteenth of September, 1978.

Illegible signature of Héctor Mario Fabbri, Officer of Vital Records and Power of Attorney.

A thick seal: Provincia de Rio Negro addressed by the Civil Registry and Power of Attorney of San Carlos de Bariloche.

Certified translation conformed to the original in Spanish *ne varietur sub*. No 81.810

He was born June 14th, 1946.
He died August 15th, 1978.
He was thirty-two.

(Didn't even make it to Jesus' age.)

Desaparecido.

It's too late.

Chapter 10
Anesthesia

How to get used to the slow strangeness [...]
of disappearance?
Éloïse Lièvre,
Les gens heureux n'ont pas d'histoire

My father's early death has always made me think history could repeat itself and, for a long time, I thought I wouldn't live beyond the age of thirty-two.

I remember that birthday coming and going, without any curse, leaving me on the other side, the side of the living, and I felt relieved, a sigh of respite, happy to be alive for my daughter, for my husband, for myself.

Today, eight years later, the doctor calls me and tells me he's found *something*.

And I imagine the worst, I envision the end, and I don't want to die of this *something*.

Weeks go by dealing with percentages, odds and statistics, appointments, analyses, and biopsies. I learn the reality of the painful vocabulary behind the TV stories of *Doctor House*. And while I wait for the foreign body to be removed, while an evil thing gnaws at me helplessly, I prepare for my death, and I cry because I'm afraid.

And I tell myself I have to write, to record, to put the words and the voice outside of me, to leave a palpable trace of my love, to leave real memories, to leave everything that I missed and I sought in vain. I tell myself that before I leave, I have to fill the space with noise, to drown the silence. I have to speak, tell, explain, show. I tell myself I don't have the right to disappear and take with me my past, my existence, my little secrets.

My daughter, my little girl, my baby,

When you listen to this recording, I'm already far away, with your grandfather, Nonno and Nonna, with Alessandro and all the others.

You must be sad, and that's normal. It'll take a while to go away, but don't let melancholy overwhelm you.

You know, even if my life has been short, it has been so beautiful. I lived trying to remember that life can end at any moment, I lived refusing boredom, I lived intensely, I loved and have been loved.

Love is the most important thing.

Who cares about work, profit, career, income? All that is just a masquerade to fill our days. They go nowhere.

What's important is to live to the fullest, let your life pulse with energy. If I could leave you with anything, it's this one and only piece of advice: don't forget to live fully.

Build a life that makes sense to you. Don't let others choose for you, listen to your core, your gut. Try not to be seduced by appealing evils. Run away from toxic people, and tell yourself that you can do whatever you want with your life.

I know you are going to get all worked up, raise your voice to tell me that I'm talking nonsense, that nothing matters because disease can catch up to us and kill us in one afternoon.

But that's exactly why you must live now, just in case. Hurry up to do whatever is on the list of things to do before we die.

Many things are still left on my list: I would have liked to visit Prague and Istanbul, I would have liked to get my driver's license, I would have liked to meet your first love, attend your wedding, hold your future child in my arms, I would have liked to do so many other things.

But that's life, my little baby, if you ever go by Prague or Istanbul, think of me…

I write this message regularly in my head, often in the evening before I fall asleep or while riding the metro. There are several variations: one in which I tell her about her birth and her childhood, another one in which I'm honest and admit that I couldn't sleep a single night for eighteen months because she was such a pain, another one in which I give her advice and tell her about my life and my past failures, another one in which I tell her the story of her father and me, another one in which I tell her about my teenage years to make her laugh. Ever since she was born, I've been telling myself I have to leave her a message.

And I don't do anything because I want to live. I don't do anything because it means that I'm giving up, that I accept my death.

I don't record myself. My daughter knows my voice.

I open my eyes in the recovery room, and I'm alive. My first thought is a feeling of guilt, of not living up to my own standards, of having left nothing, not even the password to my computer where all my memories are archived.

I open my eyes in the recovery room, and I'm alive. A woman next to me screams, she wants her mother. Another is crying in silence. Me, I'm a prisoner in a body that's slow to wake up, but I'm alive and I smile.

I open my eyes in the recovery room, and I'm alive. I am going to work hard to repair the silence, to become a family that talks to each other about everything, a family where there'll be no more masking, to not repeat history so I wouldn't hear one day *You piss me off, Maman!*

You piss me off, Maman! I'll hear my daughter's voice when she, too, starts to want answers, and I don't want to hear her voice filled with reproach and sadness. *You piss me off, Maman!* This investigation is mine, but I know deep inside that I'm doing all this for her. Asking questions, dissecting the answers, analyzing the albums in minute detail, all for her. It's too late to fill in my empty spaces, but there's still time to stop the tearing and finally stitch back together our family's history.

I saw my paternal grandmother once between 1978 and 2000. I was fifteen. After that visit, she's avoided another meet-up with excuses like the distance, the cost of an airplane ticket or our misaligned calendars. This spatial, temporal, emotional distance is what made me call her by her first name rather than grandmother.

In 2000, I decided to confront her with my existence. I took a flight and spent two weeks in a hotel a hundred yards from her home. We spent the first days in frozen courtesy, but the meetings followed one after another. Invitations to afternoon tea, lunch, walks to get a sorbet. Little by little, the ice broke to give way to a form of tenderness, and Liana finally ended her absence with a single sentence, *you look too much like my son—I couldn't stand seeing you.* She admits her cowardice, her sadness and turmoil, and she holds me tight in her arms. I know how to forgive—she's my father's mother.

We have to catch up for lost time.

I fly to Buenos Aires to ask my only living grandmother, who can speak.

CHAPTER 11
LAUGHTER

Give up your death, tinker the open fracture
of living impossibility to reduce,
to do without.
Estelle Fenzy,
Sans

Buenos Aires holds nothing exotic for me anymore. I cross the pond once a year, I rent the same apartment, I know its rooms and where things are, I shop at the Coto in San Telmo even though I prefer the one in Recoleta. I have tea at my grandmother's—to do so I take the 59 bus at the corner of Avenida Brasil and Bernardo de Irigoyen, and I get off at Ayacucho and Avenida General Las Heras. I know the streets and the shops, I greet Marciano the hair stylist, Pancho the kiosk vendor, Doña Isabel the florist. Though I'm strolling five thousand kilometers away from my house, I feel like I'm home. Buenos Aires, a city gridded with 21,013 streets and avenues that narrate a history of past splendor, avenues so long that people make appointments to meet each other at intersections: the corner of Santa Fe and Scalbrini Ortiz, Larrea and Peña, Madero and San Martín. Buenos Aires, where I wander, where my feet guide me through the chaos of the city and the *colectivos*, where every street sign reminds me that he may have walked here as well.

Sitting on the floor, listening to my grandmother talk when she's not too tired, I leaf through the albums taken out of their boxes with my head on her knee. I'm once again the little girl I should have been long ago, a little girl who should have already known all these stories.

In small brushstrokes, Franco, the favorite son, the mama's boy, takes shape. I'd had the image of a young adult, then a man, but now, I discover the playful and mischievous child, the athletic teenager, the schoolboy in a gray uniform. Photos of seaside vacations, class portraits, scenes of everyday life: the move to the house in Olivos in a northwest neighborhood of Buenos Aires, the shared garden between four attached houses, the school friends, the neighbors becoming friends, the *asados*—those spectacular barbecues, a labrador retriever. There are older pictures from the crossing between Italy and Argentina in 1947 aboard the *Tucumán*.

I plan to spend three weeks between San Telmo and Recoleta, between my apartment on Caseros Street and the one on Ayacucho Street where both my grandmother and my lemon tree live. I visit both of them every day, at tea time or lunchtime, and I make the most of the siesta hours when I rummage through armoires in search of the past. Carlos Suárez, an old neighbor and friend of the family, helps me put names to the faces in the black and white photos, then the colored photos as well.

In the evening, I consult the online archives. Day by day new technologies give me access to new documents. On the CLAMS website (Center of Latino-American Migratory Studies), I'm moved by seeing the names and the dates of boarding for both my paternal and maternal families. On the page where the Mormons strive to keep a thorough record of humanity, I find a copy of Liana Franciosa de Barendson's immigration visa with identification photo, marital status (married), the names of her parents (Michele and Nina), and her signature. I also find Nonno's. These are the puzzle pieces of a bigger picture whose shape I have yet to figure out.

I write everything down. I don't want to forget anything, not this time. I must not come back with an empty head—I want to plant our family tree.

He's growing here, in the middle of my grandmother's garden in Recoleta, a chic residential *barrio* in Buenos Aires. Tourists invade the neighborhood because of the cemetery—they come to see the tombs of celebrities, presidents, athletes, and writers. He, on the other hand, doesn't sleep in the Recoleta cemetery, he doesn't sleep between the stones, he doesn't sleep any more. He grows in the middle of his mother's garden. He's grown tall and green and, sometimes, he flowers or gives fruit. My Papa, my lemon tree, rooted in the soil of Buenos Aires, far from me, on the other side of the pond, in the other hemisphere. What will happen to my fatherly tree when grandmother passes? Will the garden be sold and the soil covered by concrete, by the dreams of a real estate developer? Will they take away my remaining roots, my last leaves?

One evening, I was invited to the cultural center in Villa Crespo, a neighborhood in Buenos Aires. My name was printed in bold above the time and date of the French Poetry event in the cultural column of the newspaper. Outsider poet, I'm an Argentinian in France who becomes French when in Argentina. I was invited to play with the languages and erase borders.

A few hours before the event, I check my email, and I turn to stone when I see a message titled: "Franco."

I barely had time to wonder what this message could tell me, didn't have time to ask if it's *Big Brother watching me*, to dwell on the probabilities, paradoxes or coincidences. My stomach ached. In almost perfect French, the message says "I knew Franco Barendson in Madrid (Spain) in 1976. Is he your parent?" and it was signed Enrique P.

Enrique P. likes poetry. Enrique P. saw my family name in the cultural column and the name brought back memories of his life in Spain long ago. Enrique P. will be in the room where I'll be giving my reading.

I then change my plan and choose to read excerpts of the work I've been writing. I translate them into Spanish, immerse myself in reading in both languages. *Me dijeron que, cuando murió, algunas partes de mi cuerpo se pusieron blancas. Me dijeron que, cuando murió, le pregunté a mi tía si ella pensaba que él estaba ahí arriba sentado en una nube [...] Me dijeron que, cuando murió, se fue al cementerio y luego a un jardín. Me dijeron que, cuando murió, se volvió un limonero.*

Enrique P. hugs me, looks at me and finds in my face my *father*'s features. He's moved, but he doesn't want to talk, not here, not like this. He tells me to meet the next day at the corner of Azcuénaga and Pacheco de Melo to chat over a *mate* and some pastries. The ache in my stomach doesn't go away, time passes slowly. Seated at a table of this *confitería* hailing from an era when my father still lived, he tells me about his friendship, the good times, the memories of his friend, his sadness, time that has passed, and life. Not much really, until the moment he pulls out two photos from his pocket showing him, his wife, my parents, and me, having a picnic on the grass in the countryside near Madrid.

He tells me, *Here,* and I cry.

I understand words cannot convey the truth, only images have this power—only pictures can attest to the existence of a man's disappearance in 1978. I want tangible proof, I want more photographs, I want all of them. Before returning home, I scan the albums and copy the labels. I even steal some duplicates of photos I found tossed in a large box. I can take the return flight in peace. I have material to fill in the family history book, I can trace my ancestry. I can finally give answers to my daughter, tell her of this grandfather who's no longer a stranger, tell her the little that I know and embellish the images with other stories I heard from all those who knew him.

Franco.

Franco was Liana's son. He ate lunch with his mother regularly and introduced her to each girlfriend-of-the-moment. He loved jewelry and gave her a gold brooch in the shape of the sun. He laughed loudly and kissed her cheeks.

Franco was the brother of Giorgio, with whom he rarely talked; Alessandro with whom he bickered non-stop; Beatrice, who was a pain in the ass for bossing him around; and Claudia, who was his favorite little sister that he joked with about the other three siblings.

Franco was once a child and not always very well-behaved. He didn't like going to school. He had lots of friends, schoolmates who thought he was a talker and the neighbor's kids who followed him around, causing all sorts of trouble. In his class photos, he wears a uniform, gray pants, white shirt, tie and a navy-blue blazer with the school's coat of arms, looking serious on the outside, a little rascal inside.

Franco was my mother's partner. He would have liked to marry her—he thought she was beautiful with her big green eyes and her lovely breasts—and he wanted to make a child with her right away. They reclined together on lawns or near pools where they went swimming. He loved making faces or mimicking someone to make her laugh, and he loved her sense of humor above everything else.

Franco had many friends, in Argentina, in Spain, in Brazil, in Peru where he once worked, in Miami where he'd gone on vacation. Their names come up from a series of photos: Ursula, Charles, Josefa, Utti, Mark, Alberto, Elsita…

Franco was my father. He often carried me on his back in a carrier and sometimes on his shoulders. He fed me with a little spoon. He lay me on his belly and gave me big kisses and burst out laughing because he was ticklish and I was squirmy. He talked to me a lot and taught me words like *cat*, *again*, *ball* or *apple*. He was lucky he lived long enough to hear me say *papa*.

Franco is now a grandfather. My daughter loves this young grandpa she can never know but who's part of her life nonetheless. I can finally tell her what a rascal he was at twelve, adventurer at twenty, traveller, painter, clown, dandy, worker, the man. I can tell her stories like the one about the monkey that came in through a window and made a mess in his wardrobe, the one about the stolen vase, or the one when he scolded me for getting out of the crib while I laughed.

Laughter is what keeps coming back when we talk about him.
Your grandfather was a man who loved to laugh.

And then my uncle Giorgio calls me. He wants to come visit on the night before my departure. On the phone he says, *It would be nice to get together for a coffee. I have to tell you something.*

What?

Chapter 12
Something

Without knowing, she knows
he held her prisoner
in his knowledge of women.
Hélène Dassavray,
C'est gentil d'être passé

I have to tell you something is one of those phrases filled with promise or terror that lovers use when they're either committing to each other or leaving. I don't want to hear anything more—my suitcase is filled with photos, I've spent hours asking a thousand questions about his childhood, his family, his fiancées, his friends, neighbors, the neighborhood, the memories. I've copied a CD with two hundred sixty-six photos between 1950 and 1960, so I can build my ancestry, a lineage, a past, a history. *I have to tell you something.*

He sits in front of me.

Words enter the conversation, float and swirl, passing from one subject to another, stopping here and there, compose meaningless phrases, words and news switch places, stretch, elongate, transform into other words. Our words over tea slip around the sofa, the cushions, between our spoons and go on and on, blah blah blah.

Words are slow to come. The words expecting to be said wait patiently while time passes and the tea gets cold.

My uncle Giorgio, my father's brother, is his opposite. He's very tall, walks with a clumsy gait. He's not very handsome, his features are irregular, and the way he dresses doesn't do him any favors—he looks like a sad and dull bookkeeper. He's not always articulate, words arrive later, after his thoughts. He looks fragile and always ready to fret about the slightest thing, as if death waited for him nearby.

So when he says he has *something* to tell me, I dread what he has to say, even expecting him to tell me of his imminent death.

Your grandfather was a harsh man.

He often took it out on your father.

Once, he even took him to the police.

At that time, we didn't know why.

We found out later on.

But we didn't want to believe it.

I don't know if I should tell you.

When you're about to hear the words that will change the state of things, your imagination opens to all kinds of disturbing and fictional images and, for a short moment, you are the daughter of a murderer, a pimp, a cannibal, your father is not your father, you are Diego Maradona's daughter, your parents were the leftist activists killed by the dictatorship, you were almost adopted by a soldier, your father snorted coke, he held up a bank in 1972 and the money was never recovered, you have a sister in Mar del Plata, you had an identical twin but she died, your father is alive and lives in Bahía Blanca where he's started a new life, your father was switched with another at birth, you were also switched at birth and your biological parents are Croatians, your father was Astor Piazzolla's hidden son…

My uncle finally articulates this *something*. I see his mouth pronouncing slowly each word so he won't forget anything, making sure that I understand what he says.

When I close the door behind him after hugging him tightly in my arms, I feel his relief. I push the door closed with my butt and slide to the tiled floor where I burst out laughing. My laughter rings through the entire apartment and echoes back to me—I have tears in my eyes. When I finish, I go to the living room, put the two cups and teapot on a tray and carry them to the kitchen. I leave dishes there and go sit on the couch with a notebook and a pen.

I put one word after another on paper, rewrite them in the new light of this other father. *You piss me off, Papa.* I had this idealized image of my father with a body, a voice, a look. I had other things besides the ashes, the soil, the tree. I had a papa, a smoker, a dandy, a player, a flirt, a painter, a car salesman, a pilot, a man. *You piss me off, Papa.* You keep on playing, you throw your cards down at the last minute, take all the winnings and laugh your ass off.

Apparently, his father found him in bed with another
man when he was fifteen.

My father was gay.

Apparently, his father found him in bed with another man when he was fifteen.

Apparently, he loved the nights in Sitges with other men.

Apparently, he and his colleague were found dead in the same bed.

My father was gay.

Apparently.

My father was a pilot.

That sounds more classy.

I laugh. I can't stop laughing. I expected anything. I foresaw the worst—I imagined something deceptive, horrible, evil. And I laugh, I let out lively and ringing laughter. I burst out laughing at this turn of events, learning my father was gay.

My uncle doesn't understand my reaction—he just told me something bad, something heavy, and I laugh again. I laugh at this refreshing news, at this snub from beyond the grave, at this great family secret now laying in my hands. I laugh to see my uncle's apologetic expression. I laugh and I don't know how to stop.

I breathe. I go back to being serious. He explains that my reaction is a nervous one. He looks for his words, tries to polish the edges, can't find the precise words, gets mixed up in paraphrases, half-words, insinuations. I see that he's fighting a strange battle between shame and honesty, and I don't know what pushed him to make this confession. Does he want to get rid of this burden? Does he want me to stop idealizing my father? Why tell me now? Why not before? Is he nearing his end?

I have to wait for him to leave so I can continue laughing.

You make me laugh, Papa.

Felipe is my best friend.

Felipe is also gay.

Felipe gets a call in the night—there's a six hour time difference, but it can't wait.

My father was gay.

He laughs.

I laugh.

Why don't I call my mother?

I grab the phone and call Felipe without hesitation. He's my friend, my confidante, the keeper of my doubts and secrets—he's been with me for almost twenty years. I laugh with him, I cry too. He knows all my weaknesses, my whims, my phobias, and he loves me for who I am. He's comforted me during my break-ups and slept in my bed to keep me company on lonely winter nights. He's the only one who shares my love of musicals and movies with Audrey Hepburn or Barbra Streisand. Together we've eaten sushi, had tea, and made fun of people on TV. So, I call him.

He's the one who tells me I should ask my mother.

It makes sense.

But I can't.

It's easier to laugh on the phone with a best friend than question my own mother.

Hello, Maman? Can you hear me? I am in Buenos Aires. I just found out my father was gay, and I'd like to know a bit more…

There are so many elements to this simple statement. I'm afraid to hurt her by telling her the man with whom she shared her life hadn't been faithful, that he preferred people of the opposite sex, told her lies on a regular basis, led a double life. How will she take it? Does she know already? Did she know then? Will she feel betrayed? Indifferent? Will she answer me? Would she consider this adultery? Is it any of my business? Will she be sad or will she laugh like I did?

I don't know her well enough to know the answers. I don't know much about their relationship, about this pair of strangers that were my parents.

I try to put myself in her shoes.

If my partner died, would I want to know this other truth?

If my partner died, would I avoid the truth, risk accidentally finding out in an awkward conversation?

People talk and lies always end up coming out, Felipe tells me.

I don't want her to think that her relationship was meaningless.

After all, I'm here.

After all, I'm the result of this unlikely union.
I don't want her to think he didn't love her.
I'm sure he loved her.
In his way.
I don't want her to doubt herself.
I don't know what I want.

My mother is a very beautiful woman. When she was young, she was simply stunning. In the photo albums, I look at her emerald eyes sprinkled with golden dots, her thick lips, her high cheeks, her long neck and the haughty way she held herself, and she could have been Dante Gabriel Rossetti's muse.

When I was in fifth grade, the boys ranked her the prettiest mom at the school. Later, in high school, all my friends fell in love with her. When I was a child, I was proud of her beauty. When I was a teenager, I envied her.

Yet my mother was shy, sometimes even insecure.
She doesn't seem to know how beautiful she is.
Or she doesn't know it anymore.
And it's his fault.
He didn't know how to desire her.
Because he preferred men.
And so she doubted herself.
Doubted her beauty, her sexiness.
How to talk to her ?
What to tell her?
Wait until the silence is broken?
Wait until the lies come out?

Ever since I've started asking questions about my father, she's been upset.

It's not about her many silences, no, it's about feeling unloved. My mother thinks I idealize my father—she thinks that suddenly I love my father more than her.

Until now, she never had to worry about my favorite parent—I've only ever had her, and I've loved her without question. Now, she thinks there's competition, an unfair fight between the living parent and the absent, dead parent.

It's nothing like that. I love her as before, as I will tomorrow. I need only to put words in the empty spaces.

Yet, there is a sort of comfort having a dead parent. You don't see him grow old. You don't witness the slow decline of his body and mind, ignore his forgetfulness, his lateness, his absences, loss of speech. You avoid conversations on pain, the doctors, the deteriorating health. You don't get the Sunday night phone calls, always sadder over little hassles, the lack of activities or friends who are sick or gone. You don't need to ask about the doctor, the pharmacist. You avoid seeing life as survival, you escape the inexorable progress towards the retirement home, the hospital, the final sleep.

That's what makes me saddest.

The day I have to witness the death of the living.

That's what makes me the saddest.

The day I have to witness my mother's death.

I needed two different tries and long pauses between to write this sentence about my mother's disappearance.

Finding my father may make this other, future death much more sorrowful.

I have to continue investigating.

Chapter 13
An Embrace, a Cold Sweat

I no longer know where you are,
and I lost your face, and your voice fades
and your body is a fiction in the night.
Herménégilde Chiasson,
Excuses

I stopped looking for Maria G. Now, I look for the men who shared a bed with my father. But I'm forbidden to ask a single question—my uncle demanded I stay quiet. He told me it's useless to question my grandmother, that she'd deny it, that my mother doesn't know, that nothing is certain, there's no proof. He tossed this bombshell in the water, so I'm now soaked head to toe and have to dry myself off and say nothing. My uncle will not talk about it anymore—the ball is in my court.

I promise silence and cross my fingers. I'll say nothing to my grandmother. She's old and doesn't like to return to sad things from the past—I don't want to make her sad. She continues to talk about her favorite son, eyes filled with tears, voice trembling. I leave her the worship of this perfect son—I keep quiet. On the other hand, I have no reason to spare my mother or my aunt.

The conversation with my mother takes place with disarming simplicity over lunch.

So you knew?

Your uncle told me two years ago.

Why didn't you tell me?

It's not up to me to tell you that your uncle thinks your father was gay.

And you, what do you think?

It's quite possible.

The conversation with my aunt will have to wait. There are some conversations you can't have over Skype.

In the meantime, I write to the entire world, to you, and I tell you *My father was gay*. I give him a universal coming out—I free his heavy secret from its cage, free his forbidden loves hidden behind a facade, from them, from their time, the country, the family, the obstacles.

When they found him dead in the hotel room, there were two men, two bodies sharing the same hotel room, two work colleagues traveling for business. A gas leak from the radiator, and they're dead in their sleep. When I was told this story, I didn't react—I took it at face value and became afraid of gas. I built a phobia that kept me away from furnaces, stoves, radiators, hot plates, Bunsen burners, anything that uses gas. I built this trauma to remind me of him, but I should have noticed their explanation was suspicious, obstructing or evasive. I should have noticed that he was found in the same bed with the other man, entangled and naked, with the smell of love, sex and sweat still fresh on the sheets.

They wanted to hide it. They wanted to avoid embarrassing the families or causing a scandal. But who made this decision? Did the hotel owner declare that he didn't want "men like that" dead in his establishment? Did the EMTs think it might be better if they separated the bodies and declared them dead separately? Did the public officer decide that it would be more decent to omit the dirty details of this sudden death out of respect for their families, especially their wives? Did the mothers-in-law bribe the public officer to not record the unfortunate truth? Did the wives know anything before? Was their death a true tragedy or a secret relief?

The man who signed the death certificate is named Héctor Mario Fabbri. He was a justice of the peace in

Bariloche province for thirty-nine years before retiring in 2012. I don't know if he's still alive, and I don't know if I could someday access the police file. I'll have to go down there, interrogate them, tell my story, and convince the official guardians of administrative memory to open the archives from a troubled time period.

What words did they use to describe the scene, to turn the clandestine lovers into asphyxiated colleagues?

Several years earlier, my grandfather found him in bed with another boy. He made him get dressed and dragged him to the police station where the chief explained that what he's done is punishable with prison time.

Sleeping with a boy is bad, it's a sin, it's a crime.

However, *in Argentina, sexual activity in the private sphere between consenting adults of the same sex has been legal since 1887.*

But he wasn't an adult—he was fifteen.
And his father didn't give a damn about laws that could feed gossip.
And the future dictator will agree with him.
And homosexuals will disappear from the country.

Did my grandfather manage to build fear in him the day he surprised him in bed with another boy? Did he fear police crackdown, or divine justice, or simply the judgement of society?

So he decided to become a lady's man to prove to his father that there's nothing to worry about, that it's all past him, that he's cured. This ensures him a certain amount of peace, and he learns to be discreet with his nighttime rendezvous.

He must have had periods of doubt, of trying to find

his identity, of shame, of excitement, of deep sadness, of loneliness and disbelief. He must have wanted to run away, to die even, and then finally found a sort of equilibrium in this double life.

The desire for fatherhood probably came later, when his age and a certain social balance allowed him to imagine being a parent.

Questions would continue to arise and never have answers, unless he met someone who'd share the secrets of his bed, unless he met someone who could have, today, become his husband.

How did he meet men? How did they understand that he was one of them? Where did they make love? Did he sleep with friends of the family? Did he have a lover, like him, who was married to one of his wife's friends? Did he sleep with other colleagues?

How many men did he know between when he was fifteen and thirty-two? How many lovers, how many one-night-stands, how many breakups, how many times did he wish he could drop everything? How many buddies did he present to the family as though nothing were happening? How many young Adonises, how many mature men, how many times, how many hotel rooms, how many apartments, how many alleyways, how many beds, how many evenings, how many drinks, how many lines, how many times?

My friend Felipe asks me if I would have been born if my father could have lived out of the closet.

I don't think it's that simple. My father always wanted to have a child. That's what everyone who knew him says. When my mother announced she was pregnant, he was thrilled. Certain it was a boy, he called me Manolo.

This arbitrary preference disappeared completely at my birth. He was the happiest father, and he said it when he wrote, *My daughter is a love.*

In one of the letters to his sister, it reads, *Someone offered us a dog, a German shepherd, called Manolo, and it is our second child (instead of having a boy, the dog will have to do). He eats everything, the furniture, the cushions, the cables, the walls, etc.*

I don't know what became of the dog. You can't see it in any photos, and nobody ever mentioned the dog to me—I thought we were a cat family.

In the end, I don't know what to think. I tell Felipe that if he could've lived out of the closet, he would've been happy with a dog that he would have named Manolo. But there are so many *ifs.*

If my grandfather hadn't barged into my father's bedroom…
If my father weren't there in that bedroom that day…
If…if…if…

No matter how many times I've questioned people, relatives, friends, family, nobody gives away anything. Everyone says he's a dandy, a player, everyone thinks he's a womanizer. I try in vain to learn his history and true nature. I keep running against a wall of taboos, a wall from a time and a country that stifles or muzzles all *deviance*, anything outside the norm. Since I made his coming out among my friends, they treat him as bi. For me, he isn't bi, he's gay, because he never had the chance to be himself, never had a place in society for someone like him.

Your grandfather was gay.
And my daughter laughs.

And if he hadn't died.
If he'd told the truth.
If he'd found love.
I could have had two papas.
You would've had two grandpas.

No big deal.

We have our lemon tree.

Chapter 14
Three Dreams, Silence

Why do we feel abandoned by the dead? Why do we blame them for their absence as if death were a choice, as if death could be avoided? He didn't kill himself. He didn't choose to disappear. He just died a stupid death. So, why the haunted nights, why this feeling of abandonment, why all this searching?

My partner understands about my anxiety better than I do and calms me down when I panic and freak out over nothing. He jokes about my fear of abandonment. He teases that he'll forget me at a highway rest stop or leave for vacation without me. Sometimes, when he's pulling the car out while I close the garage door, I feel the color drain from my face thinking he could just drive away and leave me there. He laughs and reassures me until the color returns to my cheeks. My cruel savior!

Since he's come into my life, I've almost stopped grinding my teeth at night, and if I have nightmares and wake him in the middle of the night, he takes me in his arms and holds me tightly. At breakfast, he would ask me *So? What have I done this time?* He knows that in my dreams he goes away, he disappears, he leaves me, and sometimes, he dies. He understands I'm projecting my own issues. He stays by my side, and he encourages me to search for answers.

Since I began my search, I've dreamed of my father three times. That had never happened before.

In the dreams, always the same, someone tells me he's alive and living in Argentina where he's been hiding for many years for a reason I'll learn as soon as we're reunited.

In the dreams, someone tells me that my father is on his way to see me. They give me the day, the hour, the address of a café.

In the dreams, I experience the agony of waiting for the date of our reunion. While I sit and wait, a cup in front of me, I begin to wake up. I realize that I'm in a dream, and I do everything I can to fight it. I struggle knowing there are just a few seconds left before he comes.

In the dreams, I see his silhouette down the street behind a café window. He's almost there. And I wake up in tears.

Patience. He'll get here eventually. *You piss me off, Papa.*

And this morning I saw him.
He was with my mother, and he held me in his arms.
I could barely see his face—he was far away—but I was very moved to know that at one time in our lives we were all three together as a family. I began to cry. Manon counted to three, and I opened my eyes.

Manon is a hypnotist I met at a café. I asked her naively if she could bring me back a memory from before my father's death, and she said yes.

For a month, I meet with her for an hour a week to travel back in time on her green velvet armchair.

Like everyone, I thought hypnotism was a way to create memories on your own, to convince yourself that certain images invented by the brain were real, and I was ready to make a fool of myself. But then Manon made my arm fly.

Since the first session, we haven't done much. I told her about myself, my family, this ancient death that haunts me today. She took notes, gave me some homework for the following week, and asked me to sit in the chair after trying to see if my subconscious was receptive.

Knowing if my subconscious is receptive consists of her asking me to lift my arms to touch my forehead with my index finger. My consciousness says it's totally impossible while my arm floats over the armrest. My consciousness says that I must put my arm back in its place while my hand moves towards my face. My consciousness says not to believe it while my index finger crashes into my forehead.

Glimpsing my father this morning was an overwhelming feeling. I told Manon I wanted to stop there.

I prefer the slow pace of the quest, waiting for him to come to me on his own.

People keep telling me he loved women. A lot. Too much. That's why she left him. That's what my mother says.

Even on his last night alive he tried to say he'd change, on the phone, he in Bariloche, she in Mendoza, he with his words of love, the promises he'd never keep, his desire for her, his fear of being separated from me, his reassuring words, his sweet talk, his sexy voice at the other end of the line, she with her fear of being alone, her self-respect, her barely twenty-five years and her two-year-old child, her desire for him tinged with anger, her bitterness and disappointment, her hope of seeing change, the words she wants to believe.

And a letter that he wrote once they hung up the phone, a letter found on the nightstand, ready to be sent, a letter that resumed, perhaps, the conversation on the phone, promising the stability to come, the optimistic dream of a couple in ruin.

A letter read by my grandmother.

Torn up.

Thrown out.

I was fourteen the first time I heard talk about this thrown-out letter. I was immediately enraged, a hollow burning in my stomach, a lead ball and *why* hanging suspended mid-air, until today.

I know the answer is in the letter.

I imagine a few words. I build some sentences, project some theories.

I believe less and less in the hypothesis of a reconciliation. I invent multiple versions that all seem plausible: the one where he tells her everything, the one where he leaves for Brazil to live with his companion, the one where he thanks her for her understanding over the three years of their life together, the one where he thanks her for giving him the chance to have a child, the one where he asks for custody of this child…

I also envision the worst. My father killed himself. My father wanted to abandon me.

I'm enraged by the letter's loss—why throw it away?

I decide to ask my grandmother this question. I try not to seem rude on the phone. I try to come across as naïve and relaxed in my questioning. I try not to hear the tone of accusation that quakes in my voice. I ask her why she threw out the letter. *Perché hai buttato la lettera?* Why did you throw out the letter?

She didn't throw away the letter.

She wasn't the one who took care of his things.

It was my other grandmother who claimed his belongings. My maternal grandmother, Nonna.

Stop.

What?

How?

Family members get mixed up. Some have the same first name, an aunt and a cousin, some are the same age and get confused by the older family members who can't see well anymore, and some who have the same title, like my two grandmothers.

My grandmother, Nonna, died last year. It's too late, it's always too late. To run endlessly behind this train without ever managing to climb aboard—glimpse it, reach out your hand and see it accelerate. It's exhausting.

She never told me anything. She's gone. She read it. She knew. What was she doing down there, in Bariloche? Why did she claim this letter? Why her?

I return to my mother with fresh questions. She agrees to remember—she remembers that she didn't want to go, that she didn't want to see his cold body, that she couldn't. Her mother suggested she go in her place, someone who would identify the body, sign documents, confirm his death.

I climb the stepladder. There's a big cardboard box left at the very top of the armoire. It contains Nonna's personal diary, essentially a list of where she noted, day after day, what she did, what she ate, who she saw. There are also two notebooks that she titled *A Brief History of my Long Life*. Two notebooks filled with her round and illegible handwriting, two notebooks that record her existence from 1916 to 1986. She was seventy when she decided to leave this record.

A Brief History of my Long Life is a compilation of chosen portions of Nonna's life. Both books have eight chapters and an addendum.

I. Childhood; II. Elementary School (1922-1926); III. Middle School (1926-1930); IV. Technical School (1930-1934); V. University (1934-1939) and Marriage (1940); VI. The War (1940-1945) and Emigration (1946-1947); VII. Mendoza (1947-1955); VIII. Mendoza (1956-1978); Addendum—Travel Diaries (1919-1986).

It begins with memories told by her parents. Then she recounts what she actually remembers, like a 1922 military parade. Nonna was a young girl when she found herself walking with her parents on the Vittorio Emanuele Avenue in Parma and the military passed her on the street. The man at the head of the group looked down and held her cheek. She was barely six-years-old, but she remembers the prominent jaw: Benito Mussolini. Her description of this scene is strange and ambiguous. Nonna knew what kind of man Mussolini was, but she wrote with the pitch of a child who was proud to have been noticed in the crowd.

She recounts her childhood up until high school when she met my grandfather with whom she'd spend the rest of her life. She then writes about the war, of the fear that she wouldn't see her husband return. As she remembers their moves from home to home, she draws the blueprints of the houses and the apartments she lived in. She shares recipes.

She puts notes at the bottom of the page every time she mentions a person so we can find them in the photo albums she'd numbered for that reason.

Near the end of the second book she writes, *November 4, 1978. The light that illuminated our life has been extinguished and after everything will always remain in shadow.* A few months after my father's death, my mother lost her sister. Nonna and Nonno lost a daughter. 1978: a dark year.

I imagine my mother two years earlier: this beautiful young, twenty-three-year-old woman, barely out of college with a diploma. She finds work easily, meets a handsome man who quickly suggests having a child. Life smiles. She decides to follow him to Spain, cross the ocean for a better future, raise this love child. I imagine my mother two years later: her sorrow and disappointment, her Spanish dreams buried, their separation, then the sudden and unexpected death of her partner, followed immediately by that of her sister. I imagine the darkness and the sadness that must have enveloped her heart, that aged her in an instant. I imagine all her dreams evaporating, the loss of innocence and freedom, the agony of raising a child alone, and the pain. I don't know how she built or rebuilt after that. I don't know how she was able to believe in life and navigate again toward the living. I imagine the unimaginable.

Although Nonna doesn't mention the death of my father, she implies it. *Our granddaughter, through a set of circumstances, is often put in our care.* For her, my father's death was a set of circumstances.

We are in 1986, Nonna is a young septuagenarian who sees her death nearing. She is far from guessing that she'll live another thirty years when she writes to my mother and me, *at the hour of dusk, we hope, above all, the two of them will have a future that is finally peaceful.*

And it ends like that.

There is nothing more. Not in the notebooks, not in the big box. She took it all away with her. She didn't reveal the truth before leaving. She was buried with this fucking letter, those few sentences of goodbye, of repentance, of joy, of nothing. Nothing is left but silence.

Silence.

The brief history of the short life of my father lives in words. I imagine the unspoken. I imagine the time, the place, the scene, the weather, and I imagine him, always absent.

My father is silence.

Chapter 15
A Life

I have a meeting but I won't go
I'll say that the train station arrived early.
Marlène Tissot,
Histoires (presque) vraies

Where am I supposed to look? Where can I find what I am looking for? The world seems so small when we find the same streets, same shops, same fashion styles, here and there, separated only by a few hours of flight. Information seems so accessible since the digital age, the internet links us together, webs weave between people and nations. Everything is within reach, paintings from the great masters in 3-D museums, the works of the great poets in virtual libraries, bodies of data, categorized, accessible, archives, files—but where am I supposed to look?

Until now, not a single man, not a single lover, has dared to speak up, talk about, admit, express his desire or love for him. In vain, I scour gay men's forums for mention of Buenos Aires or the beach at Sitges. In vain, I leave ambiguous phrases everywhere they can be found. In vain, I embellish the webpage dedicated to his memory with rainbow flags.

Years passed, shame fades, minds open, laws change. Men get married now, but no one comes to claim him, his past, his story. No one dares admit he's caressed his body and consumed his nights. Is it still too early, or is it already too late?

I don't know why I am looking for *the man*, this man who would have known my true papa.

I tell myself that I am looking because I want all this to be true.

My friend, Alfons, always says, "A las cosas, para que existan, se las nombra."

For things

to exist

they must be named:

My father was gay.

My father lived.

He was gay.

I continue my search, I can't help it. I can no longer be content with the few images I find. I reread the letters, I scour the internet for answers as if rubbing a magic lamp, I scrutinize the photos from my grandmother. There's this man with a moustache who appears in several snapshots. He's in a photo with my father in front of the bar he owned at Sitges. In one, with me in his arms, in another with my mother on a terrace, and another with my father again, but this time behind the counter. It looks like he was part of our life. Who is this man with the moustache?

My mother tells me he's Horacio, that he was their business associate. Together they owned the ocean-front bar, Kirikimar, in Sitges. She doesn't know his last name— she's forgotten. She thought she saw him once, in the film *Tangos: the Exile of Gardel* by Solanas. I remember this film very well, a documentary on the lives of a group of Argentinian immigrants in Paris during the dictatorship in Argentina. I fast forward through the film, looking for a moustache. I watch it again, slower, and I find the moustache. In the credits there is a Horacio A. and Horacio N. I quickly identify the first one: not him. The second one has a last name so common there are dozens with that name.

Recently, I created a page dedicated to my father on a social network. To validate the page, I had to describe my father: an artist, comedian, author, singer, musician, actor, public figure, or fictional character? After hesitating on public figure, I chose "fictional character." I got the feeling that this option would allow me to talk about all of it, to do anything at all.

On the page, there are photos, identification documents, and excerpts of letters. People are free to leave comments and are invited to share whatever could be related to my father, who materializes little by little, like in a science-fiction movie. He now has a voice, a glance, a smile, and a place where people can come see him.

The photo album grows, with photos arriving from Miami, Argentina, Florida, Paraguay, Italy, Peru, from all the places where he put down his suitcases and smiled. Women, mostly women, talk about him, his gentle manners, his humor, his zest for life, his fashion sense, his hair—about this handsome man who passed through their youth and left a tender memory. This virtual space has become a rendezvous for past friendships, a sort of intercontinental café where you run into one another, share a few words on the new generations, children, grandchildren, those who're still growing here on earth. I'm the lemon tree's daughter. People are surprised by the resemblance of my eyes, my mouth. People tell me nice things—I harvest the kindness and love of those who knew him.

I decide to upload the picture and name of Mustache on the page, even though so few people follow the site. There's my aunt Claudia, my uncle Giorgio's wife, my mother, my daughter, Felipe, my aunt's friends, some of my co-workers, a few old employees from the Braniff airline who had their own page to find fellow former employees (a sort of club that I now belong to), some friends' friends who remember him—in total a community of about thirty people.

I don't get many bites from the website: a photo of my father wearing a flight attendant's uniform, a story of a poker game, an unforgettable hangover, a letter he wrote to S. who sent it to me, specifically requesting not to be named. The letter was redacted, some passages cut, reduced to silence. I read, *My mother is true to herself, always full of mystery and scheming,* [cut] What mysteries? What schemes? Should I investigate Liana next? The letter continues like this: he says he likes it in Spain, he has a good position at SEAT, he thinks he's staying for at least five years. He adds that he envisions living somewhere else one day, but not Argentina [another cut]. What did he write? Why does S. hide it? Why did he go back to Argentina so soon after writing the opposite?

There are too many new questions. I prefer to continue looking for the Mustache. One thing at a time.

And the magic of social networks finally bore fruit.

Horacio N. writes me a message. I'm now in touch with the Mustache in the photo. Mustache lives in Paris, but he'll return to Argentina by the end of the month—I have two weeks to meet him or I'll have to cross the pond again. For thirty years, he's lived two hours away by train, and I now have only two weeks left to meet him.

I buy a train ticket.

Apparently, my father was gay.

I can't say these words over the phone. I can't write them to him. I can't talk to him about it.

I'm not ashamed. No, I'm just afraid of Mustache's reaction, this Argentinian man, this macho, Latino guy. Does he already know? Is he open-minded enough to talk about it? Did they talk about it at the time?

I send him pages of my research, pages where I search for a father, pages where I find a man who chose his own sexuality. I tell him, *read this and then we can talk about it.*

And I get on the train.

My heart and the train make the same sound.

Tatactatum, Tatactatum, Tatactatum.

I try to read a magazine, I close it, put it down, pick it up again, read sentences that tell me nothing—the words mix from one line to the next, the letters move, get bigger or disappear, I put it down, I turn it in my hands, I crumple it, I don't know what to do with my hands, my thoughts, how to put them in order, I eat, I drink, I'm not hungry, I take up the magazine again, I stare at the women, how they dress, I sweat, I drink, I feel like my hair is mussed, I want to look nice, I go to the restroom, I put on my lipstick, I'm thirsty, I walk down the aisle of the car, it sways, I have motion sickness, I don't want to sweat, I don't want to feel, I take off my coat, I sit down, I play with the magazine, I don't understand anything, I take my phone, there's no signal, I imagine our conversations, *So let's talk...So tell me... So finally someone who's known him outside of my family... So...*

I don't know why this meeting is so important. Clearly someone's opinion outside my family has more influence because it doesn't carry any emotional burden— their words have less at stake, they're more objective. My mother reproaches me for not listening to her advice and following that of my friends who, in the end, tell me exactly the same thing she did. It's as though my family's opinions need a double-check to be believed. Horacio N. is my oracle.

My heart and the train make the same sound.
Tatactatum, Tatactatum, Tatactatum.
The train arrives at the station. I set off to find out who my father was.
I have a meeting with my past.
I have a meeting with him.
Finally.
The journey reaches its end.

Horacio hugs me, tells me he once rocked me in his arms when I was just a few months old. I can't remember, but I feel good—I have a feeling that I already know him. We talk. Mostly, he talks. A lot. He talks of the past, of his arrival in Spain to flee the dictatorship that took away a sister, of exile, of his feeling of being uprooted, of the love that brought him to France, of the Argentinian restaurant he opened with his son, of his upcoming departure, of his return to the motherland, of memories resurfacing as we smile and drink on. Our words bring out more words, telling of times long ago, of beautiful women who crossed his path, of a certain Mike whose dealings landed him in prison, of his English neighbor Adriana, of the small bar he ran with my father, of how he met him, of the missed train that left him at the station at Sitges near Barcelona, of the bag filled with furs that fell off a truck, of the trade with my father (two fox fur coats for half the coffee shop shares), of my father who wanted to do business and he who wanted to start a revolution, of their fights over these differences, of the way they parted ways angry, never to see each other again.

In one of my aunt Claudia's letters, she writes *Franco was the opposite of his friends. He was practical and very concerned with money.* In the letter to S., my father writes *In winter, Sitges becomes a cemetery of writers and painters, lazy and broken people who survive as parasites off each other, and that's not how I envisioned it. The experience in Sitges has cost me a lot. The bar had been a total failure. I don't see eye-to-eye with Horacio, especially regarding money. He thinks we should let the regular customers drink for free at the bar. It's how I lost a lot of money while he gained a lot of friends.*

Horacio confirms what my father wrote. He tells me about the end of Franco's dictatorship and the freedom that came blowing through Spain, the evening discussion groups sitting on worn rugs in shared apartments, the smoke from joints that made everything a little blurry. He confirms that my father was distant from all that, that he didn't want to save the world or start a revolution—he just wanted to work so he could feed his family. Horacio has had two children since then. He tells me he sees things differently now, and he regrets the harsh words they exchanged.

So, otherwise...Did you read what I sent you?
Of course.
So? What do you think? Do you believe that...
It's beautiful, very poetic.

He didn't read it.

If he'd read it, he'd know that the little girl in front of him isn't looking for a literary opinion, but for a father. He'd know.

He didn't read it.

Or he read it, and he's avoiding the subject. He's this big mustachioed macho Argentinian man who doesn't want to talk about a man who loves other men.

Or he read it, and he's avoiding the subject. He's this proud Latino man who doesn't want any scandal, confusion, opportunities to imagine things, to get strange ideas.

Or…

He didn't read it.
We sit at a table in his restaurant. I just ate a delicious Argentinian steak with a glass of Trapiche Malbec. I lay my cutlery across my plate, and Horacio asks me if I want a dessert.

I don't want anything. I'm not hungry anymore.

This morning I left home giddy as a little girl, and now I feel old and tired. Horacio talks on, but I can only see his round face and moustache—the restaurant around us disappears in a blur. I see Horacio's lips move, smiling sometimes and even burst into laughter. I don't hear anything anymore, I nod, I smile when he smiles, I laugh when he laughs, I mimic, but I'm no longer here.

Something has shattered.

I pick up the pieces of my childish hope, order a green tea and let him know that I have to leave soon.

Horacio hugs my limp and apathetic body. I force a smile, promise another meeting in Paris or Buenos Aires. *Nos vemos.*

I just want to go home.

Strangers swarm the train station, walking like me, wrapped in their melancholy and lumpy coats, carrying heavy bags and downcast stares.

I get on the train facing the opposite direction—I don't like seeing the landscape come at me. I'm upset and my heart is cold in my tight chest. From the window, I see businessmen, couples with strollers, lovers French-kissing, excited children shouting, all like hundreds of tired, little ants pulling their rolling suitcases. The daylight fades into the evening, and the far-away scenes through the glass window lose their color, becoming a black and white movie narrated by Simone, the automated voice of the SNCF that announces departures, arrivals, and delays. Little by little the platform empties, some people run, afraid of being too late, others smoke a last cigarette, one foot on the wagon, the other foot still on the ground, the lovers don't know how to unglue from each other, and my father looks at me.

Standing on the deserted platform, wearing a navy-blue suit, a trench coat over his shoulders, he raises his hand and waves goodbye as the train pulls away and his lips mouth three syllables I guess to be *Ti amo* or *Ci vediamo*.

When I wake up, the train is rumbling on its rails. The landscape rolls by, the same meadows, the same trees I saw earlier, now swallowed by the night, replaced by the reflection of my pale face on the glass lit by neon light.

I'm tired, I want my partner to hug me. I want to sink my nose into his sweater and smell the light, pungent smell of the cigarette he smoked in secret while I was away.

Epilogue

A few months have passed and the unresolved questions don't have any answers. Two men agreed to investigate on the ground, out of kindness, but mostly for the sport of it.

Alexander has lived in Bariloche for a year, and he's spent several months looking for the records of the court proceedings by the police or any document that relates to the death of two men in a hotel. He's asked the police officers at the station, court house secretaries, the hotel employees, the local radio station, reporters at the local newspaper, *Rio Negro*, and even a certain Mr. Vilmatjana, the owner of a little shop who enjoys preserving the history of Bariloche. All in vain.

Pablo lives in Sitges and walks along the beach asking everyone. Gradually, he's gotten a few meetings: with a mafia member who couldn't tell him anything, a woman who's lived in Sitges forever but couldn't remember much, and two gay men, Paco and Mario, who remember Franco very well...his face, his smile, but that's all.

Patience.

CHRISTINE H. CHEN was born in Hong Kong and grew up in Madagascar before settling in Boston where she worked as a research chemist. Her fiction has been published in *Pinch*, *CRAFT*, *Hobart*, *SmokeLong Quarterly*, *Atticus Review*, *Pithead Chapel*, and other journals and anthologies. Her work was selected for Wigleaf Top 50, and has received Best of the Net, and Best Microfiction nominations. She is a recipient of the 2022 Mass Cultural Council Artist Fellowship and the co-translator from French of the novel *My Lemon Tree*. Her publications can be found at www. christinehchen.com

In addition to co-translating *My Lemon Tree*, M JAIME ZUCKERMAN is the author of two poetry chapbooks, most recently *Letters to Melville* (Ghost Proposal, 2018). Her essays and poems appear in *Houseguest*, *Grist*, *Fairy Tale Review*, *Hunger Mountain*, *Palette*, *Prairie Schooner*, *Southern Humanities Review*, and other journals. She is the recipient of a 2020 St. Botolph Society Emerging Artist award and has had her work featured in Boston's Museum of Fine Arts. M Jaime grew up in the woods but now lives and teaches in Boston, MA.

Samantha Barendson is a French, Italian and Argentinian poet. She was born in Spain and grew up in Mexico before settling in France. She is the author of the novels *Mon citronnier* and *Virgule*, forthcoming in 2023, and several poetry collections.

She is a Laureate of the 2015 René Leynaud poetry prize for her poem "Emergence & resistance." She received the Gina Chenouard creation grant in 2018 from the Société de gens de lettres, and a writing residency at the Villa Marguerite Yourcenar in 2019.

As a poet and novelist, she enjoys working with other artists, poets, painters, photographers, and musicians. She is a member of *Le syndicat des poètes qui vont mourir un jour* (The union of poets who will die someday) whose purpose is to promote poetry for everyone everywhere. She is also a member of *Le cercle de la maison close* (The whorehouse society) that offers performances combining poetry, music, and visual arts. She is also a member of the European *Versopolis* project. Visit her at samantha-barendson.com